Spectre

By
Keith Sadler

MAPLE
PUBLISHERS

The Spectre

Author: Keith Sadler

Copyright © 2024 Keith Sadler

The right of Keith Sadler to be identified as author of this work has been asserted by the author in accordance with section 77 and 78 of the Copyright, Designs and Patents Act 1988.

ISBN 978-1-83538-331-5 (Paperback)
978-1-83538-332-2 (E-Book)

Cover Design and Book Layout by:
White Magic Studios
www.whitemagicstudios.co.uk

Published by:
Maple Publishers
Fairbourne Drive, Atterbury,
Milton Keynes,
MK10 9RG, UK
www.maplepublishers.com

A CIP catalogue record for this title is available from the British Library.

All rights reserved. No part of this book may be reproduced or translated by any form or by any means, electronic or mechanical, including photocopying, recording or by any information storage and retrieval system without written permission from the author.

This book is a memoir. It reflects the author's recollections of experiences over time. Some names and characters have been changed, some events have been compressed, and some dialogues have been recreated, and the Publisher hereby disclaims any responsibility for them.

Contents

Acknowledgments 5

About the Author 6

Chapter One 7

Chapter Two 11

Chapter Three 27

Chapter Four 36

Chapter Five 44

Chapter Six 57

Chapter Seven 63

Chapter Eight 77

Chapter Nine 81

Chapter Ten 89

Chapter Eleven 98

Chapter Twelve 110

Chapter Thirteen 114

Chapter Fourteen 118

Chapter Fifteen 126

Chapter Sixteen 131

Chapter Seventeen 139

Chapter Eighteen 141

Chapter Nineteen 146

Chapter Twenty 149

Chapter Twenty-One 157

Chapter Twenty-Two 164

Chapter Twenty-Three 175

Chapter Twenty-Four 186

Keith Sadler

Dedication
To my father: Bill Sadler.

Acknowledgments

My grateful and sincere thanks to Butterfly, my best and oldest friend, who read the first chapter of *The Spectre* and said she was shocked and horrified that I could write a book that was so frighteningly violent, she did not want to read the rest of the book as it gave her nightmares, and she only spoke of the book because she needed to know if the serial killer is killed at the end. As I had written a horror story, I was more than pleased that she found it that terrifying.

About the Author

If I can write a novel, anybody can! I never learnt to read until I was ten years old and in my late twenties, when I wanted to be an author, I went to night school to study for GCSEs in English Language and English Literature; and I got a B in English Language and a C in English Literature. I am a retired staff nurse and in my early thirties I became an agency nurse, instead of working a permanent job, and one of the reasons was I was unable to cope with the increasing amount of paperwork staff nurses were expected to do.

I became interested in becoming a writer through watching television, as I would watch films and TV series and think that I could envisage better storylines and better plot twists and by the time I realised everybody does much the same, I was too invested in time and effort to give up.

I enjoy writing short stories and science fiction but about ten years ago a publisher told me they do not publish science fiction or short story compilations from new authors and the only genre they would publish from a new author was crime fiction and I started to write *The Spectre*.

Whilst writing *The Spectre*, I read numerous best-sellers to learn the tricks of the trade from best-selling authors.

Chapter One

He'd been stalking her for about six weeks: her name was Tiffany Bond and she was twenty-nine, blonde, and an international film star, and he was the serial killer the police and the media had nicknamed *The Spectre*. He'd been given the moniker because he had murdered twenty-one people without leaving a clue: no semen or saliva for DNA testing, no fingerprints, no footprints, no eyewitnesses, and even the criminal profilers were contradicting each other. Many crime scene investigators believed *The Spectre* was also a crime scene investigator because he was so adept at cleaning up his crime scenes.

The Spectre knew Tiffany was going to a party that evening and as she expected to be out for most of the night, she'd have no visitors until the following day and he could spend the whole night with her if he wanted to.

The Spectre gave Tiffany enough time to get dressed for the party and he then scaled the high brick wall that surrounded the huge backyard of her Beverly Hills mansion. She owned two German Shepherd guard dogs that were currently in the backyard and *The Spectre* drew his 9mm automatic pistol that had a silencer attached and shot both dogs through the head. They both fell dead without making a whimper. He then went to the back door and found it was unlocked. *The Spectre* had the know-how and the tools to pick the lock but he expected to find the back door unlocked as it was still daylight and the two guard dogs hadn't been brought into the house for the night.

He entered the house and found the housekeeper in the kitchen. Tiffany employed thirteen members of staff but as it was Saturday and she was going out, she had given them all the night off except for her housekeeper and one of her bodyguards. *The Spectre* shot the housekeeper through the head and she dropped dead almost as silently as the dogs had.

He had brought most of his equipment in a backpack, which he left in the kitchen before he started searching the house for Tiffany and her bodyguard.

Her bodyguard's name was Chuck McGregor and before working in private security, had served with distinction in the army rangers and in the Los Angeles Police Department.

"Hello," *The Spectre* said to McGregor when he found him.

McGregor was surprised into indecision for a fraction of a second and then reached for his pistol, which he carried in a shoulder holster. *The Spectre* had extensive training in unarmed combat and kicked McGregor in the midsection. As McGregor doubled up, *The Spectre* punched him in the face and knocked him to the floor. McGregor again reached for his pistol but *The Spectre* kicked him in the face and knocked him cold.

Once he'd taken care of her bodyguard, he went looking for Tiffany. He found her as she was coming down the stairs and he was speechless because she was so beautiful.

On seeing a devilishly good-looking man in her house, she assumed McGregor had let him in to see her because he was a representative from the studio she was working for.

"Can I help you?" she said with a smile, when she saw the handsome stranger was dumbstruck by her beauty, or her fame, or both.

He drew his pistol and pointed it at her. "I'm only going to rob you," he said. "If you cooperate, you won't get hurt."

The Spectre took her upstairs to her bedroom and manacled her to her bed in a spread-eagle position, using four pairs of handcuffs he had brought for that purpose. Fortunately for *The Spectre*, Tiffany slept on a bed that had very sturdy bedposts and was ideal for bondage games. He then forced a ball gag into her mouth and went back downstairs to fetch McGregor and the rest of his equipment.

The unconscious bodyguard was not a small man but *The Spectre* was able to pick him up over his shoulder and carry him upstairs to Tiffany's bedroom while he was also carrying his backpack. He gagged McGregor and cuffed his hands behind his back before he sat him in an armchair that he had already backed against a fitted wardrobe. *The Spectre* then fastened a leather belt around McGregor's neck after first threading the belt through the handles of the fitted wardrobe to ensure McGregor sat upright in the armchair and watched everything he did to Tiffany.

He then got a jug of water from the kitchen and poured it over McGregor's head to wake him up; he wanted Tiffany's bodyguard to be fully aware of how beaten and helpless he was.

The Spectre then turned his attention to Tiffany and paused to admire her beauty. After a time, he took a razor-sharp scalpel from his backpack to cut off her clothing.

Tiffany had been paralysed with fear but when she saw the scalpel, the terror within her exploded and she struggled frantically against the manacles that wouldn't yield, as did McGregor.

The Spectre again paused to watch her struggle and try to scream with a ball gag in her mouth. Eventually, she relaxed through exhaustion and he removed her shoes and started to cut away her clothing. Once she was naked, he unlocked the handcuffs, turned her over, and again shackled her to the bed in a face-down spread-eagle position. He then forced a pillow under her hips to elevate her buttocks and took a horsewhip from his backpack to beat her with.

The Spectre gave her a hard stroke with the horsewhip that left a red welt across her butt cheeks. The stroke didn't come as a surprise but Tiffany screamed and struggled as a reaction to the stinging pain.

For the next two hours, *The Spectre* fettered Tiffany in a variety of different positions, tortured her with an assortment of sadistic sex toys, and raped and sodomised her.

As soon as *The Spectre* had finished with Tiffany, he placed a plastic bag over her head to asphyxiate her. He also put a plastic bag over McGregor's head and while they were suffocating to death, *The Spectre* put on a pair of latex gloves and started to clean up the crime scene.

After about fifteen minutes, Tiffany and McGregor had suffocated to death and *The Spectre* retrieved his handcuffs and ball gags. They had both died with their eyes open, which *The Spectre* found pleasing because if people die with their eyes closed, they look as if they're sleeping, but if they die with their eyes open, they look like corpses.

The Spectre finished cleaning the crime scene and collected the bed sheet, the pillowcase, his used condoms, and anything else that had his DNA on it to take with him, and just before leaving the house, he took one of Tiffany's lipsticks and wrote on the bedroom wall in big bold red letters:

"BE AFRAID!

BE VERY AFRAID!"

Chapter Two

Dr. Dominic Blackmoor, M.D., was a forensic psychiatrist and was widely considered to be the most eminent criminal profiler in the world. To become a forensic psychiatrist, Blackmoor had first trained to be a medical doctor, had then specialized in the diagnosis and treatment of mental illness, and finally had been trained in criminology. As a forensic psychiatrist, he assessed and treated people who had committed criminal acts in which mental illness may have been a contributary factor in their crimes.

Blackmoor was frequently retained by attorneys, both for the defence and the prosecution, who employed him to assess defendants and testify in their court cases.

Blackmoor had extended his repertoire to criminal profiling when the Oregon Department of Justice had asked him to profile a serial killer they had been unable to catch, who the media had nicknamed *The Rogue River Ripper*. The naked bodies of eleven women between the ages of thirteen and fifty-seven had washed up on the banks of the Rogue River but as the bodies had been in the river for days or weeks before they were discovered, most of the forensic evidence had been contaminated or washed away.

One detective had suggested that some of *The Rogue River Ripper's* victims had been washed out to sea or eaten by river creatures and the body count could be a lot higher than eleven.

A task force was assembled after the first three bodies were found but over the next three years, eight more women were abducted, raped, stabbed to death, and thrown into the Rogue River and the police were no nearer catching the killer. In desperation, Special Agent Patrick Quinn, the head of the task force, had asked Blackmoor to profile *The Rogue River Ripper*.

Blackmoor had looked over the case files and had suggested a way they could catch the killer: he proposed creating a website that displayed much of the germane information about *The Rogue River Ripper* and an email address where members of the public could make suggestions as to how to catch the killer or nominate possible suspects. Quinn wasn't optimistic and warned Blackmoor the website would receive thousands of useless emails but as Blackmoor said he'd implement the plan himself, Quinn agreed.

Blackmoor was convinced the killer would keep abreast of the investigation and would log on to the website to see how much the police knew, and in doing so would identify himself, and the email address was purely misdirection to conceal the true purpose of the website.

Blackmoor told no one on the task force of his plan as he suspected *The Rogue River Ripper* had a law enforcement background and would hear of any initiatives in the investigation.

To upload and monitor the website, Blackmoor had employed a freelance computer programmer called Bill Dobson, who had worked for the FBI Cyber Crime Division and the National Security Agency but was now semi-retired.

Blackmoor told Dobson that thousands of people from all over the world would log on to the website but said the killer lived within the Rogue River Valley and would read all seventy-five pages of the report and not just scan a few pages and lose interest.

Dobson programmed his computer to alert him if anyone living within the Rogue River Valley viewed every page of the report, and, when alerted that someone had done so, Dobson would log on to their social media pages and learn all about them.

Within the first forty-eight hours of the website being uploaded, sixty-four people who lived within the Rogue River Valley had viewed every page of the report. Of those sixty-four, eleven were women, eighteen were schoolboys or boys under the age of eighteen, one was in a wheelchair, four had lived out of state when the murders had commenced, three did not have access to a vehicle, which would be essential to abduct the women and dump their bodies, and sixteen were retired men who were over sixty-five years old. Blackmoor agreed it was safe to exclude them, which left eleven names.

Blackmoor looked at the list of eleven names and stated: "He's in there somewhere."

Blackmoor had access to the police computer files and learnt that four of the eleven men had already been investigated by Quinn's task force and had ironclad alibis for the times some of the women had been abducted.

Of the remaining seven, three were police officers, three were journalists, and one was a private detective called Gordon McKnight. Dobson gleaned a colossal amount of information about the seven men via the internet and after Blackmoor had read all about them, he judged that the three police officers and the three journalists didn't fit his offender profile, but the more he read about McKnight, the more Blackmoor was convinced McKnight was *The Rogue River Ripper*. McKnight had been a police officer for nine years but, as a result of a conviction for the use of excessive force, had been expelled from the police force. He then became a private detective and shortly before *The Rogue River Ripper* had taken his first victim, McKnight's wife had left him and started divorce proceedings, claiming that throughout their marriage he had habitually beaten and raped her.

As soon as Blackmoor was convinced he'd identified the killer, he phoned Quinn and told him he had emailed him the name, address, and details of the man he believed to be *The Rogue River Ripper*.

Quinn had informed his task force at the start of the investigation that if the forensic evidence and the questioning of witnesses and suspects hadn't led to an arrest, the investigation was like looking for a needle in a haystack. He had extended the metaphor and said the only way to find the killer was to sort through the haystack one piece of straw at a time and criminal profiling could suggest some characteristics the killer probably had, which would narrow down the pool of suspects and indicate which part of the haystack to start looking; but Blackmoor claimed he had specifically identified *The Rogue River Ripper*.

To the best of Quinn's knowledge, in the entire history of criminology, there had never been an instance of a profiler specifically identifying a serial killer and Quinn was dumbfounded by Blackmoor's claim.

After overcoming his initial surprise, Quinn had asked Blackmoor to explain how he had identified the man he believed to be *The Rogue River Ripper* and Blackmoor had described how he had pinpointed McKnight. Quinn was sufficiently persuaded that McKnight was a viable suspect to place him on twenty-four-hour surveillance.

Three weeks into the surveillance, McKnight was seen handcuffing a young woman and forcing her into his car. When the special agents who were shadowing McKnight intervened, the young woman said McKnight had shown her a badge and told her he was a policeman. McKnight was placed under arrest and when his house was searched the police found a digital camera memory card that had pictures of all the women he'd abducted, raped, and stabbed to death. He'd taken many pictures of every one of his victims, before and after he'd murdered them, and there were pictures of thirteen women in total: the eleven the police already knew about and an additional two the police were unaware of.

Quinn was very generous with his praise of Blackmoor and said Blackmoor's input had solved the case. As a result, several law enforcement agencies had engaged Blackmoor to profile serial killers they had been unable to catch and he proved to be so adept at profiling serial killers that, as well as reading police reports, some police forces allowed him to visit crime scenes, attend autopsies, and interview suspects and witnesses.

As he often participated in investigations, Blackmoor learnt how to use a pistol and obtained a permit to carry a concealed firearm.

Blackmoor's most highly publicised case was the hunt for *The Elfin Forest Killer*, who, between 2127 and 2129, had abducted, raped, tortured, and murdered thirteen women. He had dumped their bodies in the Elfin Forest and in 2129 a rambler and his dog had stumbled onto *The Elfin Forest Killer's* dumping ground and the remains of his victims. All the bodies had been eaten by animals and were badly decomposed but most of the partial remains could be identified by dental records or DNA testing, and the two freshest bodies had evidence of being bound, tortured, and raped prior to death.

Special Agent Wayne McLintock of the California Bureau of Investigation was put in charge of the case but he was very anti-criminal profiling and wouldn't allow Blackmoor, or any of the other profilers, direct access to the investigation. McLintock had stated on the record that profilers are no better than psychics or mediums and everything they say is either stating the obvious, generalisations that are vague to the point of being useless, or guesses that are frequently wrong. He added that people vividly recall the one out of a hundred guesses psychics and profilers get right but fail to recollect the 99% of guesses they get wrong. McLintock concluded by stating: "At best, profilers waste valuable police time, and at worst, completely misdirect an investigation."

McLintock put together a task force and followed up on every lead but over the following three months another two women went missing under mysterious circumstances and it was strongly suspected that *The Elfin Forest Killer* had abducted them.

McLintock then initiated sting operations: attractive young policewomen in plain clothes patrolled the locations where *The Elfin Forest Killer* had abducted many of his victims in the hope that he would try to snatch one of them and enable the police to catch him in the act. Even though the plain clothes policewomen were carrying guns and under close surveillance, one of them went missing while patrolling a shopping mall car park.

Blackmoor had repeatedly requested to be allowed to take part in the investigation but McLintock had rejected all of his appeals, but when an undercover policewoman went missing, McLintock reluctantly agreed to allow Blackmoor to be consulted but said he would only allocate one member of his task force to liaise with him. McLintock assigned a young police officer called Jeff Sinclair, who enthusiastically phoned Blackmoor. They arranged a meeting for later that day and Blackmoor had asked Sinclair if he had any knowledge of a serial killer the media had nicknamed *The San Diego Strangler*, who had murdered sixteen people in their own homes.

The San Diego Strangler had first emerged in 2125 when he had attacked a retired couple while burglarising their home and had shot the man to death and had raped and strangled his wife.

Police investigators speculated that he may have conducted several other burglaries but this was the first time he'd used violence.

A few weeks later, *The San Diego Strangler* broke into the home of an attractive young lady and, after shooting her parents, had raped and strangled her, but he didn't steal anything of value.

In about half of *The San Diego Strangler's* home invasions, his motive appeared to be theft and the rapes and murders that accompanied the burglaries seemed to be incidental crimes of opportunity, and in the other half his primary goal appeared to be rape and murder and he would only take trophies from his victims.

Then in 2127, the murders abruptly stopped. The police believed *The San Diego Strangler* was either dead, in prison for another offence, or had relocated.

Shortly after *The San Diego Strangler's* last home invasion, *The Elfin Forest Killer* had taken his first victim, although her corpse wasn't found until 2129. Also in 2127, a burglar with a different modus operandi to *The San Diego Strangler* started robbing houses. The newly emerging burglar stole jewellery and valuable antiques, left no clues, never used violence, and could deal with very sophisticated locks and security systems. The jewellery and antiques he stole never appeared on the black market and he had apparently stolen them for his own private collection. The media had nicknamed him *Raffles* and because he was a seasoned criminal, police investigators suspected he had recently relocated to California from another part of the world and were liaising with the FBI and Interpol to try and identify him.

Blackmoor deduced that in 2127 *The San Diego Strangler* had been questioned by the police and had decided not to mix business with pleasure, and from that time had conducted his burglaries purely for financial gain and had abducted women to satiate his sadistic sexual needs and had kept the burglaries and the abductions completely separate.

Blackmoor believed that *The Elfin Forest Killer*, *The San Diego Strangler*, and *Raffles* were all the same man.

Sinclair said *The Elfin Forest Killer* had a different modus operandi to *The San Diego Strangler*, as did *Raffles*, and Blackmoor replied that both serial killers and housebreakers learn, evolve, and can respond to changes in the status quo.

He asked Sinclair to get the suspect lists for all three investigations and said the man they were looking for would be on all three lists, would be a minor suspect in *The Elfin Forest Killer* and *Raffles* investigations but would have become a major suspect in *The San Diego Strangler* investigation shortly after the last home invasion had occurred.

All three lists had thousands of names on them as everybody who was ever questioned or connected with the investigations, no matter how briefly or trivially, was placed on the suspect lists. Sinclair ran all three lists through the computer and 1954 names occurred on two of the lists, 127 names occurred on all three, but only one man was a minor suspect in the *Raffles* and *The Elfin Forest Killer* investigations and a major suspect in *The San Diego Strangler* investigation: a man called Grant Hobson.

Hobson was a minor suspect in the *Raffles* investigation because he owned a company that installed security systems and panic rooms and he had the expertise to carry out the burglaries. Coupled with that, Hobson was a part owner of a firm that bought and sold gold bullion and one of the police investigators had suggested that *Raffles* was melting down the jewellery and antiques he had stolen and selling the gold bullion through a legitimate business. This was thought to be unlikely as most of the value of the jewellery he had stolen was in the gems and not the gold, and most of the value of the antiques he had stolen was in their age and scarcity and not in the weight of the gold they were made of, and the meltdown value of the gold, for both the jewellery and the antiques, would be a fraction of their original value. Also, *Raffles* often stole antiques that were not made of gold.

He was a minor suspect in *The Elfin Forest Killer* investigation as geographic profilers had worked out from the locations the women had been abducted, and from the place he had dumped their dead bodies, that *The Elfin Forest Killer* probably lived within a certain area of San Diego County and owned a vehicle big enough to transport his victims, as did Hobson and a few thousand other men.

Hobson had become a major suspect in *The San Diego Strangler* investigation shortly after the last murders had occurred as the police had discovered that the owners of three of the houses that had been invaded by *The San Diego Strangler* had had estimates for home security systems from Hobson's company, and in all three cases, Hobson had been to the houses to give the estimates. Hobson had agreed to be questioned without a lawyer present and had consented to his home, his place of work, and his vehicle being searched without a warrant, and as no incriminating evidence was unearthed, the police focused their attention on other suspects.

Sinclair met with Blackmoor, armed with all the data about Grant Hobson on a laptop computer.

"He's our man," Blackmoor said after reading the reports. "Let's go straight to his house."

The Spectre

"We don't have probable cause," Sinclair said.

"We won't need any," Blackmoor replied. "Hobson will be extremely cooperative, as he always has been in the past, as being completely cooperative is the best way to minimise police suspicions."

Sinclair drove to Hobson's big expensive house, which was surrounded by a high brick wall and had CCTV and electronically controlled gates.

After Sinclair had pressed the intercom buzzer five times with long pauses in between each buzz, Hobson spoke to them over the intercom: "What do you want?"

"I'm a police officer and I'd like to ask you a few questions," Sinclair said.

The electronically controlled gates swung open and Sinclair drove into Hobson's driveway.

As the gates closed behind his car, Sinclair realised no one knew they were there, and if Hobson murdered both he and Blackmoor, no one would ever know, and Sinclair radioed his control centre and informed them where he was and what he was doing.

Hobson met them at his front door and had just begun to invite them into his home when he recognised Blackmoor and was momentarily taken aback. Blackmoor had written and presented a six-part television documentary series about forensic psychiatry and was frequently recognised by members of the public. Most people who'd seen Blackmoor on TV didn't know he was a forensic psychiatrist and thought he was a classically trained actor who'd been employed to present the show. It was an easy mistake to make as Blackmoor had a movie star's good looks, was only twenty-eight when he'd filmed the show but looked even younger, and, as a psychiatrist, had worked long and hard to perfect a demeanour that was empathic and charming. After making the documentary series, he had been offered several gigs presenting other television documentaries that were not within his sphere of expertise, but, although Blackmoor enjoyed the fame, forensic psychiatry was his passion and he declined all the offers. He had even been offered an acting role: a major film studio was planning to remake *Gone with the Wind*, an epic historical romance film set in the American South during the American Civil War and the subsequent reconstruction, which tells the story of Scarlett O'Hara, the beautiful daughter of a Georgia cotton plantation owner, and Rhett Butler, a blockade runner for the Confederacy. Rhett Butler loves Scarlett O'Hara but she is in love with another plantation owner called Ashley Wilkes. The casting director thought Declan Lee was the obvious choice to play Rhett Butler, as he was the most bankable leading man in Hollywood at that time, his signature role was Robin Hood, and he had played a dashing lovable rogue in about half a dozen other blockbuster movies. The casting director was looking for an actor who was even more handsome and charismatic than Declan Lee to play Ashley Wilkes and had suggested Dominic Blackmoor to the director and the producers. They thought it was an intriguing idea and had invited Blackmoor to audition for the role but he had declined the offer.

"Dr. Dominic Blackmoor!" Hobson said after he overcame his initial surprise. "I watched every episode of your show; I thought you were very good."

"Thank you, I'm flattered," Blackmoor replied.

Hobson invited them to be seated in his living room and offered them tea, coffee, or a cold drink.

"We're investigating *The Elfin Forest Killer*," Blackmoor said.

"How can I help?" Hobson asked.

"We'd just like to look in your safe room," Blackmoor replied.

The firm Hobson owned installed a variety of security systems, including safe rooms, or *panic rooms* as they were more commonly called, which were designed to hide and protect their occupants. They were constructed with concrete walls that were reinforced with steel sheeting and had a steel door with a keypad-controlled electromagnetic lock. Secrecy was frequently part of their defence and the rooms would be sound-proofed and the steel doors would be hidden behind sliding wall panels.

"We interviewed one of your employees and he told us he'd worked on a safe room in your home," Blackmoor quickly added before Hobson had time to deny he even had a safe room in his house. Blackmoor was bluffing and he hadn't spoken to any of Hobson's employees, but Hobson didn't know that.

"Do you have a search warrant?" Hobson asked.

"Do we need one?" Blackmoor replied.

"I use it to store junk that I no longer need but that I don't want to throw away," Hobson said. "I hardly ever go to my safe room, and on the rare occasions I do, I can never remember the code to the keypad, but I've got it written down somewhere."

Hobson looked pensive for a few moments and then started searching through the draws of a bureau he had in his living room. Then suddenly, he snatched a .45 calibre automatic pistol from a draw and shot Sinclair in the chest. Hobson was turning to shoot Blackmoor, when Blackmoor shot him twice through the heart and once through the head in quick succession, the way he'd been trained. As Hobson staggered backwards and slid down the wall, Sinclair shot him three more times in the torso.

Sinclair had been wearing a bulletproof vest and was in shock but was not injured.

They called for backup and while they were waiting, they searched for Hobson's safe room. They found it hidden behind a sliding bookcase but they were unable to open the steel door. Backup arrived and they called in some of Hobson's employees to gain entry to his safe room. It took Hobson's own crew about two hours to get the door open and to the surprise of some of the police officers, and to the great relief of them all, they found the undercover policewoman alive. She'd been raped and tortured but she was alive.

Hobson was using his safe room as a torture chamber and evidence discovered there, including a laptop computer that had dozens of recordings he'd made of the sadistic sex games he'd played with the girls he had abducted, proved he was in fact *The Elfin Forest Killer, Raffles,* and *The San Diego Strangler.*

Blackmoor's profile of Hobson was so incredibly accurate that some criminologists had suggested that Blackmoor and Hobson were a team of serial killers and that Blackmoor had shot Hobson to death before he had time to talk.

As a result of being the world's premier offender profiler, Blackmoor had a large fan following and some of his devotees believed he had ESP and used his supernatural powers to hunt down serial killers. Blackmoor had no psychic abilities but the truth of how he identified serial killers was perhaps even more mysterious and sinister. The cliché that serial killers make the best profilers was very true of Blackmoor and he craved to be a serial killer but had always kept his sadistic and homicidal impulses under control. As he had stated in the television documentary series he had written and presented:

We all experience violent or socially unacceptable impulses to a lesser or greater degree but most of us exercise self-restraint and have a sense of right and wrong and feelings of compassion for the suffering of others.

And Blackmoor did have a code of honour and feelings of compassion, although he didn't believe he experienced compassion as deeply as most other people experience it.

Blackmoor counselled and treated other profilers, forensic psychiatrists, and law enforcement officers, as a great many of them had developed emotional problems, including depression, night terrors, and mood swings, as a result of getting into the minds of serial killers, sadistic psychopaths, and other criminals, but Blackmoor thrived on it and voyeuristically studying and hunting serial killers, satiated a deep need he had to be one himself.

Blackmoor thought his method of profiling was analogous to the methods used by an art restorer called Kevin Boscastle, who

The Spectre

said before he could restore an artist's work, he would first have to get into the artist's heart and mind. Boscastle's most challenging assignment had been to restore the work of a painter called Marcel Jacques Carpentier, who was the most famous painter of his time and was as well-known as Picasso and Rembrandt. Carpentier had said that throughout his life he had striven for perfection in his art and had only achieved perfection thirty-one times, and he had kept those thirty-one paintings for himself and he wouldn't sell them, exhibit them, allow anyone to take photos of them, and had only allowed a very few select people to even look at them. Shortly after his death, his latest wife, who was over thirty years his junior, had expected to inherit his entire fortune, but, although she had been left well provided for, he had divided his estate amongst his ex-wives, his lovers, and the many children he had fathered in and out of wedlock. Carpentier had left his thirty-one most cherished paintings, which had been estimated to be worth millions, to his eldest daughter, who had given him five grandchildren. In a fit of jealousy, his latest wife had poured paint stripper over each and every one of his thirty-one beloved paintings. Some of the paintings were largely intact and others were almost completely destroyed, and Boscastle had been employed to restore them. He began by interviewing everyone who had seen the paintings and he made some sketches based on their recollections, and while he was making the sketches, he studied every one of Carpentier's paintings, and there were hundreds. Boscastle then started restoring the thirty-one pictures, beginning with the least damaged one and concluding with the most badly damaged one, and after eleven months, he had restored all the paintings. They were put on display in the Louvre and art critics unanimously said that Boscastle had just painted his own pictures on Carpentier canvases and it was a Boscastle exhibition, not a Carpentier exhibition.

A couple of years after Boscastle had completed the restorations, a lifelong friend of Carpentier's had died and his next-of-kin had found a video recording of Carpentier's thirty-one most treasured paintings that had been made before they had been damaged and restored, and Boscastle's restorations were so incredibly accurate that art critics said Boscastle must have channelled Carpentier's spirit. And in the same way that Boscastle got into the hearts and minds of other artists, Blackmoor got into the hearts and minds of other serial killers.

Blackmoor was currently profiling a serial killer the police had named *The Spectre*, who had murdered twenty-four people.

The Spectre had first struck in Miami when he had killed an illegal arms dealer called Miguel Camacho, as well as seven of Camacho's bodyguards and Camacho's current trophy girlfriend. His bodyguards had been shot, but Camacho had been overpowered in hand-to-hand combat and then bound and made to watch while his girlfriend had been tortured and raped. He and his girlfriend were then both murdered by suffocation with plastic bags over their heads and 'BE AFRAID! BE VERY AFRAID!' had been written on the wall in her lipstick.

The police had first thought that Camacho and his team had been taken out by a squad of rival gunrunners, as they didn't believe one man would be capable of taking out eight well-armed, highly trained, battle-hardened mercenaries, but Miami crime scene investigators said all the slugs and spent cartridge cases came from just one gun: a 7.5mm Caledfwlch Assault Carbine. The police then theorised that a high-end contract killer had been employed to eliminate Camacho and his crew.

Seven weeks later, *The Spectre* resurfaced in New York and murdered a champion mixed martial arts cage fighter called Kirk Bulmer, four of Bulmer's sparring partners, and Bulmer's sexiest groupie. Bulmer's sparring partners had been shot with a 9mm automatic pistol, and not the 7.5mm Caledfwlch Assault Carbine that had been used in Miami, but investigators believed it was the work of *The Spectre* as other features of his modus operandi were present: Bulmer had been overpowered in hand-to-hand combat, he had been restrained and made to watch while his sexiest groupie was tortured and raped, they were both murdered by suffocation with plastic bags over their heads, and 'BE AFRAID! BE VERY AFRAID!' had been written on the wall in her lipstick.

There were allegations that Bulmer had been using performance-enhancing drugs and as he had hospitalised and maimed several of his opponents, the injuries he had inflicted during contests could be regarded as criminal assaults, and the media had speculated that *The Spectre* was a fanatical vigilante.

The Spectre had gained a comic book hero status in some circles, but he then resurfaced in Las Vegas and murdered a policeman called Gavin Fairfax and Fairfax's wife and four children. Fairfax was an ex-Navy SEAL who had served with distinction in South America and Africa and, after leaving the Navy SEALs, had joined the Las Vegas Metropolitan Police Department and became a SWAT Team Leader, and his police record was as distinguished as his military career. His wife had once been Miss Nevada USA, and she could have represented Nevada in the Miss United States of America beauty pageant, but she had given up her modelling career to be a housewife and mother.

The Spectre's latest killings had been in Los Angeles, where he had murdered a movie star called Tiffany Bond, her housekeeper, and her bodyguard.

Blackmoor had read all the forensic reports, visited all the crime scenes, studied the lifestyles of all the victims, and had then profiled *The Spectre*:

The Spectre is a sadistic psychopath with a narcissistic sense of entitlement and a grandiose sense of self-importance. He is in his thirties, highly intelligent, a martial arts fanatic, and is dominant in the S&M scene with both submissive partners and sex workers. He is an international entrepreneur and his ruthless, competitive, ambitious, deceptive mindset has made him a very successful businessman. The focus of his attacks has been physically powerful men and their attractive female partners and the other people murdered at the crime scenes were collateral damage. Although he enjoys the torture, the rape, and the complete domination, humiliation, and the eventual murder of his victims, his primary goal is the fame and the fear his crimes inspire, which is why he writes, 'BE AFRAID! BE VERY AFRAID!' on the walls of his murder rooms and why he specifically targets physically powerful men.

Chapter Three

In his capacity as a forensic psychiatrist, Blackmoor had gone to the Orange County State Hospital for the Criminally Insane. The Orange County State Hospital for the Criminally Insane had had quite a few high-profile inmates over the years but its most famous resident had been a serial killer called Geraint Taunton. Taunton's modus operandi was to torture, rape, and murder people in their own homes and then burn down their houses to obliterate any forensic evidence. Because fire was part of his signature, he had been given the epithet *Satan*.

Taunton had been involved in a road traffic accident when he was two years old, in which both of his parents had been killed and he had been left with considerable facial scarring. It was widely believed by psychologists and criminologists that if it had not been for that traumatic event, Taunton would probably not have become a serial killer.

Taunton was an author who had written fifteen bestselling novels before he was caught and another eighteen bestsellers while incarcerated and had won many awards, including a Nobel Prize for Literature. He also wrote screenplays for the cinema and for television and was even more celebrated as a screenplay writer than as a novelist.

Taunton had always declined to give interviews or to make guest appearances in any of the films or TV shows he'd written, and the only exception he had ever made was to appear in a phenomenally successful and long-running television series he'd authored called *The Dark Ages of Gorrgon*.

The Dark Ages of Gorrgon was a sword and sorcery show set on another planet and had a great many intertwined plots and subplots. Taunton had based one of the storylines on William Shakespeare's play *Macbeth* and the character based on *Macbeth* went to a castle dungeon and explained to about a dozen of the vilest outlaws in the kingdom that he wanted to employ them to do some wicked and evil things that his own troops might refuse to do.

The leader of the outlaws replied:

The cruelties and injustices of this life have robbed me of any feelings of humanity or pity I might have had and have deprived me of any feelings of guilt or remorse for anything I do to spite the world.

After reading the script, the director had asked Taunton to play the leader of the outlaws and Taunton had agreed. Taunton said he had agreed to play the role because he had developed a lot of respect for the opinion of the show's director but all of Taunton's biographers, and there were many, believed Taunton had played the leader of the outlaws because he had based the character on himself and the speech was autobiographical:

The cruelties and injustices of this life have robbed me of any feelings of humanity or pity I might have had and have deprived me of any feelings of guilt or remorse for anything I do to spite the world.

The critics were as impressed with Taunton's acting as they were with his writing and the show's producers, fans, and director all urged Taunton to reprise the role and give the character a larger part in the next season, and, after some persuasion, Taunton had agreed.

Taunton hadn't given the character a name during his first appearance on the show but the fans had named him *Geraint*, because that was the name of the actor who had played him, and Taunton thought that name was as good as any.

The storyline for *Geraint's* return was a baron had employed him as a spy and an assassin and *Geraint* had proved so skilled at both that he was soon the baron's spymaster. As the spymaster of a powerful baron, *Geraint* had a taste of power and money, and all the privileges that come with both, and he wanted more.

The Spectre

Taunton often borrowed ideas from the plays of William Shakespeare when writing the screenplays of *The Dark Ages of Gorrgon* and he had based some aspects of the plot of *Geraint's* reappearance on *Richard III*. During Shakespeare's play, *Richard* referred to his ugliness and deformities and affirmed that was the cause of his inhumanity and malice (a concept which Taunton almost certainly identified with) and Taunton repurposed, adapted, and modernised many of *Richard's* soliloquies for *Geraint*, who repeatedly referred to his own hideously disfigured face.

Geraint frequently shared his thoughts and feelings with the audience by means of a voice-over and as the viewers could hear what he was thinking and he spoke directly to them, it gave each and every one of the viewers a sense of being *Geraint's* best and only friend:

In place of conquest and the murder of rivals, which I excel at, the barons are extending their influence and forming clan alliances with marriages. And as I have a hideously scarred and disfigured face that both frightens and disgusts, and as I am not of noble birth, I am of no use in such matters. Should I return to poverty and insignificance while the ungrateful warlord I made rich and powerful discards me, or should I use the lessons a lifetime of pain and suffering have taught me to gain high office?

Some people thought borrowing ideas from Shakespeare was almost sacrilege, others thought it was a tribute to the Bard, but most people who expressed an opinion on the subject, including English teachers, classically trained actors, and drama critics, thought Taunton had outdone the master.

Taunton was also a student of martial arts and had studied numerous styles of combat and became an expert in many of them. As a result of his studies, he had compiled the most extensive video library of martial arts in existence and had video recorded experts from all over the world, demonstrating and describing their styles of combat.

Blackmoor was at the Orange County State Hospital for the Criminally Insane to assess a man called Garth Johnson. Johnson had been the right-hand man of a religious cult leader called Joshua Owen, who was in the ilk of Charles Manson and Jim Jones. Blackmoor had first crossed paths with Johnson when the parents of a nineteen-year-old girl had approached him and said their daughter had joined Owen's religious sect and had asked Blackmoor to get her back for them. Blackmoor had some experience with cults and interventions and had devoted an episode of the show he'd written and presented to the subject (which was why the girl's parents had contacted him in the first place) and after researching Owen's religious sect, he was convinced that Owen was exploiting his followers and was responsible for a great many crimes up to and including murder.

Blackmoor had told the girl's parents to send an email to their daughter stating that a distant relative had died and had left her a lot of money and that she had to go to a lawyer's office to collect a cheque. Owen had sent her to the lawyer's office and had also sent Johnson and another three of his henchmen to escort her. Blackmoor had already asked the local police for their assistance and had asked them to take any guards that came with her into custody so he could get her away from them. Getting the girl away from Owen's strong-arm boys wasn't as much of a problem as Blackmoor and the local police had thought it would be, as when the police checked them out, they found Johnson and his three cohorts all had outstanding arrest warrants in various parts of the USA. Once her four guards had been arrested and removed, Blackmoor reminded the girl that Owen had instructed her to get the cheque and he took her to her family home and engaged her in conversation. Blackmoor had told her parents that if he could talk to their daughter, he could assess if she had been brainwashed and, if so, he could start to deprogram her. He also wanted to get information about Owen's cult and she told him stories of people being compelled to sign over all their money and property to Owen, of people being held at Owen's isolated religious retreats against their will, of people being used as slave labour, and, most significant of all, she told stories of people who had mysteriously vanished. Blackmoor gleaned enough information from the girl for the police to obtain warrants to search Owen's religious communities and for a forensic accountant to go through Owen's financial records. Police investigators soon unearthed a mountain of incriminating evidence, including several dead bodies, and Owen and several of his minions were arrested.

Johnson was facing numerous charges, including assault, kidnapping, rape, extortion, and five counts of murder.

Johnson and his attorneys had said he had been brainwashed by Owen and had been compelled to do those evil things, and Blackmoor had been appointed by the court to assess the validity of his claim.

Before meeting Johnson, Blackmoor had read the police reports, the court transcripts, and the reports written by the psychiatrists employed by Johnson's lawyers. The psychiatric reports started with his childhood and said his father had abused him physically and psychologically and had abandoned him when he was fourteen. Johnson had then survived by begging, petty theft, and being an underage prostitute, until he encountered Owen, who became a father figure to him. Even as a teenage boy, Johnson had been quite tall and a mean street fighter and Owen had sent him to train at martial arts clubs and weight training gyms with the intention of making him a bulwark of his organisation.

Johnson's lawyers had also noted that since Johnson had been away from Owen's influence, he had cooperated with the police, he had expressed remorse for the vicious things he had done, and he had been a model prisoner.

When Blackmoor interviewed Johnson, the hospital staff were alarmed at how lax Blackmoor was about his own safety: the hospital staff were called nurses but their standard operating procedures more closely resembled prison guards and they had put manacles on Johnson's wrists and ankles, but Blackmoor had insisted that the manacles be removed and that he be left alone with Johnson. The only security measure Blackmoor would allow was some nurses could wait in an adjoining room.

"What can I do for you?" Johnson asked courteously once they were alone, sitting down, and facing each other across a table.

"Your lawyers are claiming Owen brainwashed you and compelled you to commit the violent crimes you're charged with and the court has asked me to assess the validity of the claim," Blackmoor said.

The courts frequently employed Blackmoor to conduct psychiatric assessments of defendants and he fully understood that he had little or no reason to believe anything the criminals he interviewed said, as psychopaths can be very convincing liars and being a forensic psychiatrist didn't make him a mind reader. Many psychopaths deny any involvement in the crimes they have committed, some boast they have committed crimes they had nothing to do with for the fame and for the glory, some invent or embellish stories of abuse they'd suffered as children to gain the sympathy of the court, and some pretend to be mentally ill because they'd rather be incarcerated in a mental hospital than in prison.

"I first met Owen when I was fourteen," Johnson said. "I was homeless and hungry and wandered into one of his missions."

Johnson was now twenty-seven, six feet three inches tall, and had a physique like a bodybuilder, and Blackmoor had trouble picturing him as a starving fourteen-year-old boy.

"Owen garnered a great many lost souls," Blackmoor replied. "Most of them became victims but you became a victimizer."

"Owen sized up everyone he met," Johnson said. "And he quickly figured out I'd be more used to him as a wolf than as a sheep and he said I was going to be one of his bodyguards."

Blackmoor agreed that Owen was a confidence trickster and, as with all good conmen, he could assess people very quickly and work out who were gullible and who were the vulnerable. Blackmoor also agreed that as a cult leader, Owen needed a crew of henchmen, whom he referred to as *bodyguards*.

"You have bisexual tendencies?" Blackmoor said.

"I've raped both men and women if that's what you're asking me," Johnson replied. "But Owen knew rape was an effective way to coerce people and he ordered me to do it and said it was God's work."

For the next forty-five minutes, they discussed Johnson's upbringing and his abusive father, his experiences on the streets after his father had abandoned him, his relationship with Owen, and the brutal things Owen had instructed him to do.

"As a reward for loyal service, Owen had let me use recreational drugs and had told me to take any members of his cult I wanted and use them in any way I liked," Johnson said. "I took both men and women of all ages, body types, and ethnic groups, I experimented with every kind of fetish imaginable, and, when Owen told me to, I tortured people to death."

Johnson had admitted to nothing that wasn't already on the record from multiple statements made by many members of Owen's cult and Blackmoor thought that everything Johnson had said so far had been rehearsed with his lawyers.

"I've been interviewed by an author who wants to write a book about me," Johnson said. "And he told me a major Hollywood studio is making a film about Owen's cult and they want the actor who's playing me to be the central character. I have a large fan following and the old proverb that *bad men do what good men dream about doing* is very true."

Blackmoor thought it was unlikely that Johnson had rehearsed his last statement with his defence attorneys and was surprised that Johnson had gone off script.

"All kinds of people ask me about the things I've done, and not just my fans but lawyers, policemen, doctors, even a Catholic priest who wanted to convert me to Catholicism and take my confession," Johnson said. "They ask me about the drugs I've used, the kinky things

I've done, or the murders I've committed, and by what they want to hear about, I know what they fantasise about doing themselves. People go to see a movie or a sporting event so they can live out their fantasies by watching a movie star or a professional athlete do the things they'd like to be able to do themselves, and people who haven't got the brains or the guts to do the things I've done, get their kicks by listening to me talk about it."

Suddenly, Johnson was interrupted by an emergency siren. All the staff carried personal alarms (a small hand-held electronic device that emitted a loud alarm siren when activated) and the siren meant there had been a violent incident, usually a patient attacking a member of staff or another patient, and all available staff had to go and deal with the emergency.

"All the staff on the other side of that door have gone to deal with an emergency," Johnson said. "If you scream for help, there's no one out there to hear you."

With one sweep of his arm, Johnson sent the table that was in between them flying across the room.

Blackmoor gathered that Johnson had suppressed his sadistic and homicidal urges since his arrest and he was now unable to keep them bottled up any longer, even if it meant spending the rest of his life in prison. Blackmoor also gathered that Johnson intended to beat him, anally rape him, and then murder him.

As Johnson stood up, the handsome young man's facial expression changed from a reassuring smile to an intimidating glare and his tallness and broad shoulders gave him the bearing of an ogre. Members of Owen's cult had reported that Johnson could change from charming to terrifying in the blink of an eye and now Blackmoor fully understood how true their reports were.

As the hulking brute lunged at Blackmoor, Blackmoor threw him to the floor with a ju-jitsu technique.

"You've studied the martial arts," Blackmoor said. "So have I."

The Spectre

Johnson quickly got to his feet and attacked his smaller opponent with a combination of karate techniques. Blackmoor blocked or evaded all of Johnson's kicks and punches and then counter-attacked with a roundhouse kick to his body that fractured three of Johnson's ribs and a punch to his face that broke Johnson's nose and knocked him flat on his back.

"I'm going to tell the court that, in my opinion, Owen influenced you to do his dirty work but he selected you more than brainwashed you, because he'd deduced that you're a sadistic psychopath," Blackmoor said. "I agree that bad men do what good men long to do, but good men exercise restraint."

Johnson slowly got to his feet and picked up the chair he'd been sitting on, which had been knocked over in the fight, and, after repositioning the chair, sat down.

"So, what do you want me to tell you about?" Johnson asked.

Blackmoor also picked up his chair and sat down and was very tempted to ask Johnson about the murders he'd committed, but as he was presently Johnson's psychiatrist, Blackmoor replied: "What would you like to tell me about?"

Chapter Four

Blackmoor had arrived early for his 3 pm appointment with Jonathan Huxley, the Los Angeles County District Attorney, and was waiting patiently outside of his office. Huxley, and many of the other lawyers at the District Attorney's Office, frequently consulted Blackmoor in his capacity as a forensic psychiatrist, but Blackmoor had no idea why Huxley had made an appointment to see him that afternoon.

At 3pm Blackmoor was escorted into Huxley's private office and Huxley invited him to be seated.

"How well did you know Professor Dean Ambrose?" Huxley asked as soon as they were alone.

Professor Dean Ambrose was a forensic psychiatrist who had died just over a year ago. Like Blackmoor, he had worked for the FBI and had counselled traumatised law enforcement officers but he was most well known for being the author of a book called *The Making of Monsters*, which outlined the genetic and environmental elements that create serial killers and was essential reading for all criminologists.

"He was a friend and a colleague of both of my parents," Blackmoor replied. "And he was a mentor to me since I made the decision to specialise in forensic psychiatry."

Blackmoor's father had been a consultant psychiatrist and his mother had been a professor of child psychology and both of his parents had collaborated with Professor Dean Ambrose on several projects.

Blackmoor and Huxley had both attended Ambrose's wake and Ambrose had left instructions that he wanted an unattended cremation and that his ashes be scattered in his back garden while his friends had drinks and snacks. He also specified that he wanted an afternoon gathering and not an all-day affair that went on into the evening.

This was exactly the arrangement Blackmoor would choose for himself if he ever found the time to leave instructions.

Ambrose had no children and had outlived his wife and all his siblings and had left his house and everything he owned to his housekeeper, apart from a very generous gratuity that he'd left to his gardener; Ambrose loved his garden but hated gardening, which was something else he and Blackmoor were like-minded about.

Ambrose had requested that Blackmoor be the one who scattered his ashes and although Ambrose had requested an unattended cremation, Blackmoor had gone to the crematorium to ensure that Ambrose's body was treated with respect, and, even though the crematorium delivered the ashes, Blackmoor insisted on transporting the ashes himself.

"Dean Ambrose was a close friend and a confidant of mine for many years," Huxley continued. "And since his death, I've been at a loss for someone to talk openly with, and I'd like you to take over as my counsellor."

Blackmoor was initially surprised by Huxley's request but he quickly processed the information and responded: "Of course I'll be your counsellor; we can start now if you like."

Blackmoor usually conducted counselling sessions while he and his patient were sitting in armchairs as that generally made his patients feel more at ease, but if Huxley felt more relaxed sitting in an office chair with his desk in front of him, Blackmoor would comply.

Huxley immediately commenced their first counselling session and was pleased to be able to do so: "After I graduated from law school, everyone I knew just assumed I was going to be a corporate lawyer: partly because they couldn't imagine me in a courtroom and partly because corporate law was where big money was to be made. But I became a prosecutor because I wanted to stop bad men."

Blackmoor mused to himself that ninety-nine out of a hundred people who work in law enforcement, originally did so to make the world a better place, and he would have said so if they were just having a friendly chat but he believed that 90% of psychotherapy was being a good listener.

"I've also been politically active on quite a few occasions," Huxley said.

Blackmoor was aware that Huxley was considered to be a political guru and that his opinion on political issues was greatly valued and highly sought after, especially in California. Blackmoor was also aware that many attempts had been made to cajole Huxley into running for the governorship of California himself, but he had always declined to do so, stating that he supported policies, not people or parties, as far as it was humanly possible, and if he ran for office himself, he would lose his neutral overview of political situations and his opinions would have to be biased in favour of the party he was representing.

Huxley had compared the political process to the legal process and said the politicians on either side of a debate are comparable to the prosecution and defence lawyers in a court case and both politicians and lawyers give biased viewpoints to sway the opinions of the voters or the jurors, but, as he wasn't a politician, he could give an unbiased overview of any proposed policy, he could clarify the advantages and the disadvantages of the proposed policy, and he could give a personal opinion, if he had one.

"When I was a young deputy district attorney, I campaigned for Justin Llewellyn when he ran for the governorship of California," Huxley continued.

As a Californian, Blackmoor was well acquainted with Justin Llewellyn's political career, and, like Llewellyn and Huxley, Blackmoor was an incrementalist.

Justin Llewellyn was a professor of history at the University of California and he had written a book about politics called

An Evolutionary, not a Revolutionary. Llewellyn proposed that, whenever possible, political innovations should be implemented on a limited trial basis and if they work, keep them and expand on them incrementally, and if they fail, rescind them. He gave several historical examples of evolutionary and revolutionary political and social changes and made a few suggestions about possible changes for the future.

One of his suggestions, which became a major policy in his bid for the governorship of California, was the state control of recreational drug distribution. Llewellyn commenced his line of reasoning by pointing out that the police had been waging an ineffective and expensive war against recreational drugs for decades and argued that if recreational drugs could not be eliminated, they had to be controlled.

The first step of his plan was to open a single cannabis bar, which would be based on the coffee shops in Amsterdam where cannabis was bought, smoked, or eaten if it was sold as an edible. If cannabis was only sold at a single bar and the sale of cannabis in any other context was made illegal, its effects could be accurately monitored, and if it proved to be doing more harm than good, the cannabis bar could be closed down, and if it proved to be solving more problems than it caused, it could be expanded on and other cannabis bars could be opened. Llewellyn added that even if the state control of cannabis distribution proved to be a success, it would still require some fine-tuning as there were dozens of different types of cannabis.

Regarding heroin and cocaine, Llewellyn noted they were a great deal more dangerous than cannabis, and many people become addicted and have their lives ruled and ruined by them. For that reason, they should not be sold in establishments that have a seductive ambience, as are alcohol, tobacco, and cannabis, and they should only be sold in state-controlled centres that have a clinical environment. And before buying heroin or cocaine, the customers would be compelled to watch a truthful but horrific information film about the dangers of using such drugs, and the staff at the centres would be trained and equipped to enable the users who became addicted to detoxify and rebuild their lives.

Llewellyn predicted if recreational drugs were state-controlled, it would save billions of dollars of taxpayers' money that was being spent on an ineffective war against drugs, it would eliminate the spread of HIV and hepatitis caused by the repeated use of contaminated needles, it would control the quality and quantity of the drugs and prevent deaths and injuries by contamination and overdose, it would take away the huge black market profits from organised crime, and several foreign despots who finance their fiefdoms and private armies with money they make by producing and selling narcotics in the USA would lose much of their income, power, and prestige. He added that organised crime and police corruption go hand in hand with enforcing silly laws and the example he gave was the prohibition of alcoholic beverages in the 1920s, which led to gangsters known as *bootleggers* illegally smuggling and selling alcohol and having gun battles with rival gangsters.

Llewellyn said he strongly believed the state control of recreational drugs would be a success but added he couldn't be certain until it had been tried and tested, and as he had stated in his book: *As every research scientist would confirm, the outcome of an experiment is never certain until it's been carried out, but politicians are expected to be supremely confident as to the outcome of their policies to the point of possessing a crystal ball or a magic wand.*

"The state control of recreational drugs was of particular significance to me because as a young deputy district attorney, I frequently had to prosecute drug addicts and I didn't think sending them to prison was the best thing to do with them," Huxley said.

Llewellyn served two terms as the governor of California and the state control of recreational drugs proved to be as successful as he had predicted: the number of people who became unemployed, homeless, hospitalised, imprisoned, or deceased as a result of recreational drug use went down dramatically; the police didn't have to investigate, arrest, and prosecute drug addicts and the criminals who supplied them with drugs, and it relieved pressure on the police, the law courts, the prison service, and the taxpayers; and, even after running costs, the cannabis bars and the narcotics dispensing centres turned a profit for the taxpayers who financed them.

It proved to be so successful in California that other states in America, and other nations worldwide, introduced the state control of recreational drugs.

Many experts were of the opinion that alcohol and gambling were as addictive and dangerous as narcotics and a few lobby groups were campaigning to make alcohol and gambling state-controlled.

The Democratic Party had asked Llewellyn to be their presidential candidate but he said a great deal of politics at the presidential level has to be urgent and pervasive responses to crisis situations and he liked gradual changes not radical ones and didn't consider himself to be up to the task.

"Many years later, I campaigned for Sheila Jefferson when she ran for the governorship of California," Huxley said. "She proposed that if someone wanted a licence to carry a pistol for self-defence, they'd first have to go through a training programme that was as rigorous as the police have to. Sheila said the extensive training programme would greatly reduce the number of people who were killed or injured in accidental shootings and muggers would be reluctant to attack strangers, as they could never be certain who was carrying a concealed pistol and had been trained to use it."

Sheila Jefferson was a retired police officer who never rose above the rank of sergeant and had spent most of her police career behind a desk. She had little experience in politics and if Huxley hadn't campaigned on her behalf, it was very unlikely she would have won the election, and Blackmoor had heard rumours that she and Huxley were lovers.

Blackmoor vividly remembered that Sheila Jefferson's amendment to the law regarding a citizen's right to carry a concealed firearm received a lot of affirmation after a man called Paul Howlett went on a killing spree at a busy theme park. Paul Howlett had had a long string of jobs that he had lost as a result of his bad attitude and disrespect of his colleagues and employers, the last of which was as a cleaner at the theme park where he went on a killing spree. He owned several guns, both legal and illegal, and he returned to the theme park on a busy Saturday afternoon, armed with a hunting rifle, a submachine carbine, an automatic pistol, and a rucksack full of ammunition. Howlett had written in his journal that he intended to walk through the theme park and slaughter as many people as he could before he was killed in a shootout with a police SWAT team. He opened fire with the submachine carbine on the packed ranks of people who were queuing to enter the theme park and killed eleven people and wounded seventeen more before he was shot dead by a forty-seven-year-old postal worker called Graham Wells.

A number of postmen had been mugged, as the muggers were hoping the postmen were delivering parcels or letters that had money or valuables in them, and this had prompted Wells to complete the extensive pistol training course, obtain a licence to carry a concealed weapon, and buy a pistol for self-defence. He was at the theme park with his daughter and three grandchildren when Howlett had opened fire with his carbine, and Wells had drawn his pistol and shot Howlett dead. The police estimated that if Howlett had walked through the theme park shooting people as he went, the death toll would have been well into three figures, many of whom would have been children.

"One day I hope the USA will be as gun-free as Britain, where guns are almost impossible to obtain illegally, where very few people own firearms, and even the police do not need to routinely carry guns," Huxley said. "And Sheila's amendment to the law regarding a citizen's right to carry a concealed firearm was a step in the right direction. As Llewellyn had defined it: *Social and political changes often require a considerable amount of time to be implemented to enable people to recalibrate their norms and become accustomed to the reforms.* It took decades, if not centuries, for Americans, both black and white, to become accustomed to racial equality, and it will probably take equally as long for Americans to become accustomed to not owning guns."

Over the next hour, Huxley talked about many of the people he had prosecuted and said the fear of losing cases and letting violent criminals loose on society was his constant companion, and that trepidation was only surpassed by the dread he had of sending innocent people to prison.

Huxley's comments put Blackmoor in mind of a quotation by the British philosopher Bertrand Russell: *The trouble with the world is that the stupid are cocksure and the intelligent are full of doubt.*

Chapter Five

It was Friday evening, the beginning of the weekend, and Blackmoor was looking forward to spending time with his friends. Blackmoor, as a renowned consultant forensic psychiatrist, had to be professional, formal, and guarded with almost everyone he met, and his friends were the few people he could be himself with.

His best friend was a man called Toby Shackleton, who had once been an army combat medic and had seen action in South America and Africa. Toby had said he believed most wars were either dynastic dogfights, armed robbery on a grand scale, conquest and occupation to enslave indigenous populations, or, worst of all, genocidal extermination of entire ethnic groups to recolonize their lands. When Blackmoor had pointed out to him that joining the armed forces and believing that all wars were immoral seemed paradoxical, Toby said he had wanted to do something to make the world a better place and being a combat medic in war zones seemed to be the best way of doing it. He explained that as well as giving medical care to wounded American and allied troops, he had also treated wounded enemy combatants and injured civilians. Toby had compared himself to a German businessman called Oskar Schindler, who had collaborated with the Nazis during World War 2 but had only done so to save Jews from the gas chambers by claiming he needed them to work in his factories. Toby had added that World War 2 was fought to crush the Nazis in Germany, the fascists in Italy, and the military dictators in Japan, and he said he would have fought in that war.

After being honourably discharged from the army, he worked as a paramedic and did a lot of voluntary work for the homeless of Los Angeles, who reminded him of the war refugees he had helped in South America and Africa. The homeless of Los Angeles were people who had rejected conventional society or who had been excluded from it, like the chronically mentally ill, parole violators, teenage runaways, alcoholics, and drug addicts.

Toby said he'd like to make sweeping changes to make the world a better place, as had Norman Borlaug or Bruce Willoughby, but he was doing the best he could with the limited talents he had.

Norman Borlaug was a biologist and Nobel laureate, who had introduced hybrid cereal crops into agricultural production in Pakistan, India, Mexico, and other developing countries and had saved over a billion people worldwide from starvation.

Bruce Willoughby was an irrigation engineer and Nobel laureate, who had lived at the time of global warming when deserts were expanding, droughts were becoming more frequent and severe, the polar ice caps were melting, and sea levels were rising and flooding many coastal regions. Willoughby had diverted water from the great rivers of the Earth to irrigate deserts and parched farmlands to supply food and water for a still expanding human population and, by retaining water from the world's great rivers on dry land, had saved some coastal areas from flooding.

Blackmoor vividly remembered the first time they'd met and the first thing Toby had said to him: *I work with the homeless and I think one of my co-workers is a serial killer.*

Toby immediately had Blackmoor's undivided attention.

Toby explained that several young ladies had disappeared and were last seen in the company of a volunteer called Cedric Dunn.

Dunn had been working with the homeless of Los Angeles for a lot longer than Toby and when Toby had discussed his suspicions with a couple of other volunteers who had worked with the homeless for even longer than Dunn, they said it wasn't unusual for homeless people to suddenly move on, but now Toby had made them think about it, they recalled quite a few attractive young ladies who had suddenly vanished after last being seen with Dunn.

Toby had clandestinely followed Dunn to his house, which had a large backyard that was surrounded by a high fence. Toby had climbed the fence to view Dunn's backyard and had observed that Dunn had planted several trees in straight lines and the spacing of the trees resembled tombstones in a graveyard. Toby had surmised that Dunn had planted trees on top of the corpses of the women he'd slain, partly as a pretext to dig deep holes in his backyard and partly to commemorate the murders. The trees would also mark where the bodies were buried and enable Dunn to make full use of available space and ensure he didn't dig up one corpse while burying another. So far, Dunn had planted fourteen trees.

After verifying that everything Toby had told him was accurate, Blackmoor concurred with each and every one of Toby's conclusions and approached the LAPD and proposed they bait a trap for Dunn with an undercover policewoman. They selected a policewoman called Victoria Buchinski, who approached Dunn at the homeless shelter with a cover story that she was a battered wife on the run from an abusive husband. Dunn immediately offered to let her stay at his home, in his spare room, and they went to Dunn's house in his car.

Buchinski was carrying a concealed radio transmitter and was being shadowed by a police SWAT team.

On reaching his house, Dunn had asked her to make herself comfortable in his living room while he went to make her a hot drink and something to eat. He quickly returned and was armed with a taser (an electroshock weapon): the model of the electroshock weapon Dunn was armed with fired two fifteen feet long wires that were tipped with barbed electrodes that could penetrate clothing and skin and deliver an electric shock that caused neuromuscular incapacitation and rendered the victim helpless.

As soon as Buchinski saw the taser, she screamed as a signal to summon help from the police SWAT team that was shadowing her. As Dunn took aim and pulled the trigger, she raised her handbag as a shield. The barbed electrodes harpooned her handbag and didn't harm her. After a couple of seconds of surprise, Dunn pounced on

Buchinski and tried to strangle her but she had been extensively trained in unarmed combat and had overpowered Dunn before the police SWAT team had entered his house.

The police searched Dunn's house and discovered that he had had the basement soundproofed and had equipped it so it could function as a prison cell, including a steel ankle manacle that was linked to a long heavy-duty chain that had been bolted to the wall, suggesting Dunn had imprisoned his victims for a time before he had murdered them.

The police also found fourteen storage boxes that contained the personal belongings of the fourteen women he had murdered, which Dunn had probably kept as trophies.

Crime scene investigators then excavated the trees in his backyard and found the remains of a woman under every single tree.

Whilst being questioned, Dunn said his modus operandi was to stun his victims with an electroshock weapon, and while they were helpless, he'd carry them to his basement, strip them naked, and fetter them with either ropes or chains; the level of restraint he used would depend on how physically powerful the woman he had ensnared appeared to be. Once the women were naked and fettered, he'd beat and rape them, and if he couldn't beat and terrorise them into complete subservience and they kept resisting him, he referred to them as *sex toys* and he'd strangle them and bury them in his backyard after a couple of days. If he could beat and terrorise them into being completely subservient, as was the case with most of the women he had ensnared, he referred to them as *sex slaves* and he'd keep them for a few weeks before he disposed of them.

Victoria Buchinski, the policewoman who had gone undercover to catch Dunn, was a sergeant in an LAPD SWAT team and was another of Blackmoor's close friends. She allowed none of her colleagues to call her by her first name and they called her *Buchinski, Sergeant,* or *Sarge,* depending on their rank and the context they were addressing her. In Blackmoor's opinion, the old cliché that a woman working in a male-dominated profession has to be twice as good as any man doing the same job just to break even was exemplified by Buchinski. Buchinski, like Blackmoor, had to play a role, and Blackmoor and their four mutual friends were the few people she could be unguarded with and she allowed them to call her *Vikki*.

The fourth member of Blackmoor's band of close friends was an ATF Special Agent called Iain McNaughton. Iain was tall, broad-shouldered, and had a couple of ugly facial scars, all of which gave him an extremely menacing appearance. Iain had been a Green Beret and, after leaving the Special Forces, had joined the Bureau of Alcohol, Tobacco, Firearms and Explosives.

The fifth member of the band was a woman called Cheryl Koenig, who was also an ATF Special Agent. ATF Special Agents frequently disarm and arrest gunrunners and militia groups, and these arrests often become hostage or siege situations, and Cheryl's primary role was as a hostage negotiator. Blackmoor had seen Cheryl in action and she was the best hostage negotiator he had ever known. She had also been trained as an interrogator and she was also unsurpassed at that, although she had the advantages of being female, extremely attractive, blonde, and having big blue hypnotic eyes. Iain had been trained as an interrogator by the CIA and he and Cheryl frequently worked together as a *good cop, bad cop* team.

The sixth member of the band was a black man from Detroit called Martin Luther Hadleigh, or *Marty* as he preferred to be called, who, like Blackmoor, was a martial arts fanatic.

Blackmoor had studied numerous styles of unarmed combat and had been taught by several martial arts instructors but his greatest influence was Geraint Taunton. Blackmoor had read everything Taunton had ever written about martial arts and had obtained copies of the video recordings Taunton had compiled of many of the world's greatest martial artists of his time.

Taunton had mastered many of the traditional oriental styles of combat and, according to legend, could effortlessly switch from karate to Tai Chi and from Tai Chi to ju-jitsu. Taunton had said every style of combat has its advantages and disadvantages, and as he had studied most of them, he could quickly discern an opponent's strengths and weaknesses.

Blackmoor had developed his own style of unarmed self-defence and had noted there were hundreds of styles of combat, thousands of techniques, and an infinite number of combinations of techniques, and some very exceptional people, like Taunton, could master a great number of them, but lesser mortals could only master a few, and the fewer techniques a student tried to perfect, the better he could become at those limited number of techniques.

Blackmoor also noted that many styles of combat require years of uninterrupted training before a student was skilled enough to use the complicated techniques in a street fight and he began his teachings with techniques that were comparatively easy to learn, perform, and retain without continual practice.

He taught beginners grappling techniques, largely borrowed from wrestling, as most street fights, especially for beginners, quickly became close-quarter contests. Blackmoor then taught his students short strike techniques, largely borrowed from boxing.

Blackmoor had added that, in his opinion, the most valuable aspect of martial arts training was *fear management,* and unarmed combat training enabled the students to become accustomed to fighting and to be unafraid of fights, and he gradually introduced his students to fighting with wrestling matches, followed by short strike technique sparring.

Blackmoor initially employed a grading system from white belt to black belt, and the dress code of his style of self-defence was a gi (a lightweight two-piece white suit traditionally worn when training in karate, judo, and other oriental martial arts), but he had changed the dress code from a gi to anything his students found comfortable, and he himself usually wore jogging bottoms and a T-shirt. He retained the colour-coded grading system, but in place of belts, Blackmoor used head and wrist sweatbands with his club insignia stitched onto them.

Blackmoor predicted that some of his students would wear the sweatbands when not training, which would demonstrate that they had trained in unarmed combat and could be perceived as bragging and might provoke confrontations. To negate this, Blackmoor suggested that his students only wear sweatbands while training and take them off as soon as they had finished the lesson. He himself only wore a single wrist sweatband and most of his students followed his example. This, in turn, led to another innovation: Blackmoor had asked one of his students what his grade was and the student had displayed his wrist sweatband by clenching his right fist and slamming his fist against his breastbone. The habit quickly spread and Blackmoor had decided to use it as a salute to replace the traditional bow.

Marty had urged Blackmoor to introduce dan grades but Blackmoor said he used a colour-coded ranking system to give his students a sense of accomplishment, and once his students had reached black band level, they would study purely for the love of the art.

Initially, Blackmoor had taught all the classes himself, but as his style of unarmed self-defence became increasingly popular, and he became ever busier, he employed some of his black band students to teach some of the classes for him. The number of people who wanted to learn his style continued to grow and Blackmoor had made some of his black band students into *Instructors*, which meant they could start their own clubs and grade up to the black band, and to identify he had made them into *Instructors*, he gave them black sweatbands with white edges.

To maintain the integrity of his style, Blackmoor had intended to grade all the *Instructors* himself, but because the number of people who wanted to learn his style of unarmed self-defence had snowballed, he had empowered Marty to teach and grade *Instructors* and he had introduced new black sweatbands with midnight blue edges to identify that the wearer was an *Instructor of Instructors*. So far, Blackmoor and Marty were the only *Instructors of Instructors*, but Blackmoor knew he'd have to make some more if the number of people who wanted to learn his style of unarmed self-defence continued to snowball.

To earn the first grade, the yellow band, in addition to learning some grappling techniques and short strike techniques, a student would also have to learn some moral codes of behaviour. Blackmoor didn't expect his students to become philosophers, psychologists, or Buddhist monks, but he taught them not to be bullies or braggarts. He taught them only to use violence in self-defence or to protect the weak and that any kind of bragging was a putdown, and for a martial artist, humility is equally as important as courage.

As his students progressed through the grades, he taught them a basic knowledge of all the major styles of combat and then encouraged them to choose, practise, and perfect the techniques they found most appealing.

When Blackmoor had decided to employ some of his black band students to teach some classes for him, the first person he thought of was Marty. Marty's family were very pleased when he'd started working for Blackmoor as, for once, he had a full-time job with good pay: Marty had only worked part-time jobs since he'd left school to free up time to enable him to study the martial arts and as soon as he was proficient enough, he had worked as a self-defence instructor, a bouncer, and he had even had a few mixed martial arts cage fights, but his skills in the martial arts had never paid off until he'd started working for Blackmoor.

Marty had wanted to give Blackmoor's style of unarmed combat a name and Blackmoor wanted to call it *The KISS Self-Defence System*, *KISS* being an acronym for *Keep It Simple Stupid*, but after a lot of debate, they agreed to call it *The Blackmoor-Taunton Self-Defence System*.

A sociologist called Professor Elizabeth Barrington-Smythe had predicted that the style of self-defence Blackmoor had pioneered would become increasingly popular and would eventually have more of an impact on society than everything else Blackmoor had done, even though Blackmoor had made significant contributions to humanity as both a forensic psychiatrist and as a psychologist. She noted that in addition to teaching moral codes of behaviour as an essential part of his self-defence system, Blackmoor also taught how diet and exercise could be used to prolong life and delay the ageing process, and his teachings had more of an influence on the lifestyles of the people who studied them than did many of the world's major religions and political ideologies.

Blackmoor and his five closest friends would frequently spend time together at each other's homes or would train together at dojos, gymnasiums, or shooting ranges. That evening, they met up at a high-class Beverly Hills sports centre, where most of the patrons were the Los Angeles rich and famous. Blackmoor could afford membership as he was a bestselling author, a consultant psychiatrist, and a TV personality, and he could sign in his five best friends. Blackmoor had taken his friends to an expensive sports centre as Vikki and Iain frequently took him to shooting ranges that were exclusively for law enforcement personnel and he felt he needed to make it up to them. They worked out in the weight training gymnasium for a couple of hours and after showering, they went to the sports centre's health food restaurant to eat, drink, and gossip.

At the end of the evening, Blackmoor drove Vikki to her apartment and she invited him in. They were lovers in a purely physical relationship, or *fuck buddies* as Vikki defined it, and they also played sadomasochistic role-playing games. Vikki was the submissive and their safe words were *Green Light*, *Amber Light*, and *Red Light*. *Green Light* meant start or harder, *Amber Light* meant ease up but don't stop, and *Red Light* meant stop. As with all S&M role-playing games, *the submissive is always in control,* and there was an absolute rule that the safe words, especially the one to stop, had to be obeyed.

They had three favourite role-playing games: *The Spoilt Brat*, *The Stuck-up Bitch*, and *The Irresistible Temptress*.

As *The Spoilt Brat*, Vikki would wear a schoolgirl's uniform consisting of a pleated miniskirt, black seamed stockings and a suspender belt, tight white panties and a matching bra, a white blouse, and a necktie. Once she'd said *Green Light*, Blackmoor would play a disapproving adult and would put her across his knee and spank her bottom. While spanking her, he would tell her she was naughty, lazy, disrespectful, and a dirty little slut. Vikki would protest the punishment was unjust, she was too old to be spanked, and that she'd been disciplined enough. She'd then plead with Blackmoor to stop and tell him how painful the beating was, but he wouldn't stop unless she said *Red Light*.

As *The Stuck-up Bitch*, she'd wear a business suit and behave very arrogantly, and while Blackmoor was disciplining her, she'd be outraged and threaten vengeance.

As *The Irresistible Temptress*, they never needed safe words as she would simply tell Blackmoor what she wanted him to do to her and he would lavish her with compliments while doing it.

Blackmoor fully agreed with a sex therapist who said: *Sex without foreplay is like buying an expensive bottle of vintage wine, pouring it into a beer glass, and drinking it in one breath.* And as Blackmoor was into bondage and corporal punishment, the foreplay could go on for hours.

"Make yourself comfortable while I get changed," Vikki said as she entered her bedroom.

While she was changing, Blackmoor waited with keen anticipation as he pondered what she might wear. Since the beginning of her affair with Blackmoor, she had collected an assortment of erotic lingerie, and Vikki was attractive enough to be a fashion model and curvaceous enough to be a glamour model.

When she finally emerged from her bedroom, Blackmoor was trembling with excitement.

Vikki had decided to play *The Stuck-up Bitch* and was wearing a blue business suit with a tight skirt that emphasised the roundness of her hips.

"Green Light," Vikki said.

Blackmoor was waiting for her in her living room and she expected him to drag her to the couch and put her across his knee, but he picked her up over his shoulder and started carrying her back into her bedroom.

She gave a short involuntary scream of surprise and then said: "Put me down, you brute!"

Blackmoor didn't put her down as she hadn't said *Red Light* and instead gave her a hard slap across her bottom.

"How dare you!" Vikki responded.

Blackmoor sat on the corner of her bed, put her across his lap, and started to spank her across the seat of her tight skirt that had been stretched even tighter when he had bent her over his knees. As it was the warm-up phase of the spanking, Blackmoor was slapping her quickly but with little force. He routinely began corporal punishment sex games with a tantalizing mock spanking even if the submissive he was dominating favoured a hard thrashing.

"That's awful, you Neanderthal!" Vikki protested as she frantically kicked her legs from the knees and sent her shoes flying through the air.

After about fifty smacks, he rolled her onto her back, laid next to her on his side, and used his body to hold down her left arm. He then reached under her head with his right arm and seized her right wrist with his right hand. Once he'd pinned down Vikki's arms, he unbuttoned her jacket and blouse with his left hand while she pretended to struggle. As soon as he'd undone all the buttons, he rolled her onto her front and pulled off her jacket and blouse. He then unbuttoned and unzipped her skirt and pulled it down.

She was wearing black panties with a matching bra and black seamed stockings and a suspender belt, which she knew Blackmoor liked. Vikki usually wore black stockings because Blackmoor thought they were the most erotic, but for variety, she occasionally wore red, white, or blue stockings and while doing so she would wear a bra, panties, and suspender belt of the same colour.

Blackmoor paused to admire how beautiful Vikki looked in her erotic underwear and then started to fondle and pat her buttocks. Vikki had a very sexy butt and he couldn't fully appreciate how perfect it was unless she was lying face down. He petted and patted her bottom for a time and then continued to spank her on alternate butt cheeks.

After about every fifty smacks, Blackmoor would make the spanking a tad harder, and every time he made the spanking harder, he'd leave a longer period of time between smacks, as the harder he slapped her, the more it would hurt and the longer it would take for the pain to fade away, and he allowed her more and more time to fully enjoy the sting. Vikki closed her eyes to focus her attention on the pain and yelped with delight after every smack. Her yelps of pleasure could be interpreted as outrage for the purpose of the role-playing game, which thrilled both Blackmoor and Vikki.

For the fourth time, Blackmoor made the spanking a little harder, and after he'd given her the first hard slap, he waited to see if she'd say *Amber Light*, which meant she wanted him to continue with the spanking but not so hard, but she screamed: "Ouch! Stop it you son-of-a-bitch, that hurts!" as she kicked the bed from her knees.

Blackmoor again raised his hand and brought it down with a loud slap on her bottom.

"Ouch! I'll get you for that you bastard!" she screamed.

Blackmoor gave her about a dozen hard spanks with long pauses between smacks, and Vikki protested and kicked the bed throughout.

"Red Light," she finally said when she'd had enough spanking.

Blackmoor unhooked her bra strap, flipped her onto her back, and snatched off her bra. Her breasts were as magnificent as her buttocks. He then seized her wrists, held her arms down in a spread-eagle position, and gently bit her breasts as if he were a toothless baby breast feeding, and every now and then, he'd gently chew her nipples.

Blackmoor was pretending to rape Vikki and the safe word to make him stop still applied but she enjoyed being taken by force as long as it was part of a role-playing game and she was the one who had chosen the role-playing game scenario in the first place.

Her eyes rolled back in her head and she intermittently struggled against Blackmoor's hold-down. At times she'd struggle because it thrilled her to feel that Blackmoor had overpowered her and at other times she'd struggle because she was delirious with ecstasy and she'd try to hug Blackmoor as an involuntary response to his lovemaking. Vikki never grew tired of this, so Blackmoor continued for quite some time.

Eventually, he stopped, rolled her onto her front, and sat astride her thighs. He did this to free up his hands so he could take off the rest of his clothes and put on a condom while he was still holding her down. Blackmoor then gave her one last pat on her bottom before he snatched off her panties, which were very wet at the crotch. While she was lying face down, he grabbed her wrists, held her hands level with her hips, and bit her butt cheeks the way he'd bitten her breasts. He then rolled her onto her back, again seized her wrists, held her hands level with her hips, and licked, kissed, and gently bit her vagina. Vikki was delirious with ecstasy and she screamed and struggled uncontrollably against Blackmoor's hold-down until she'd climaxed. Blackmoor wanted to make Vikki climax twice and he again held her arms in a spread-eagle position and mounted and penetrated her. Vikki needed a lot of work to reach a second climax and as Blackmoor was close to finishing, he had to close his eyes and think of the most disgusting things he could imagine to delay his orgasm. Eventually, Vikki started to scream and struggle and when he knew she was close to climaxing, he opened his eyes and allowed himself to focus his attention on how beautiful she was and they climaxed together.

Chapter Six

The following Sunday morning, Blackmoor met with Toby, as Toby had asked him to help with some voluntary work he was doing for the homeless of Los Angeles. A camping and outdoor equipment store was closing down and the owner had offered any unsold stock he had left over to a homeless shelter where Toby did a lot of voluntary work. Toby jumped at the offer as warm, waterproof outdoor clothing would be invaluable to the homeless. The owner's only condition was the store had to be cleared by Monday morning, before the new owners moved in, and Toby had borrowed a truck to transport the goods.

A man called Jack Smith, who was living at the homeless shelter that the outdoor equipment had been donated to, had volunteered to help, and after they had loaded all the goods into the truck, Toby, Blackmoor, and Jack climbed in and sat amongst the equipment.

The truck was hydrogen-powered and was designed to be eco-friendly and only produced heat and water as by-products. The truck was also self-driving and was steered by a computer that had a speech recognition facility, which Toby instructed to drive to the homeless shelter. Almost all vehicles in modern industrial nations were hydrogen-powered and driven by a computer with a speech recognition facility, including police and emergency vehicles like the ambulance Toby used as a paramedic.

Blackmoor had been studying Jack Smith and he was proving to be an enigma. Unlike most of the homeless people Blackmoor had encountered through Toby, Jack was bathed and his clothes were freshly laundered, although he wore well-worn work clothing. He had an athletic physique, which suggested he worked out regularly, and while they were loading the camping and outdoor equipment into the truck, he displayed a lot of strength and stamina. One of

Blackmoor's many influences was Dr Joseph Bell (1837-1911), who emphasized the importance of close observation and deductive reasoning in making a diagnosis and was Sir Arthur Conan Doyle's inspiration for the literary character Sherlock Holmes. Blackmoor had taught himself to use close observation and deductive reasoning to analyse the people he met but Jack was a puzzle to him and defied his Sherlockian reasoning: Jack made an effort with his personal hygiene and his physical fitness but lived at a homeless shelter and wore old second-hand clothes.

"I watched every episode of your TV show," Jack said. "At the shelter I was staying at when your shows were first broadcast, the television was in the communal hall and you had quite a following."

"I'm flattered," Blackmoor replied.

"You said serial killers make the best profilers, because it takes one to know one, and you and one of the serial killers you've profiled should go on *A Mile in His Moccasins*," Jack continued.

A Mile in His Moccasins was a television series in which two people swapped jobs. The show's title was taken from an old Native American proverb that said, *"You should never judge a man until you've walked a mile in his moccasins."*

The first show in the series featured a drummer in a rock band, who, via the internet, frequently criticised the teaching skills of his school music teacher and, in response, his music teacher had said anyone could learn to play the drums well enough to perform in a rock band within a week. For the purpose of the show, the drummer had a shave and a haircut, put on a suit, and taught schoolchildren music, and the music teacher put on a wig, a false beard, and dark glasses and played the drums in a rock band. After six weeks, the drummer realised teaching music to children wasn't as easy as he had thought it would be, and the music teacher said he'd never imagined what a buzz playing the drums in a rock band was and, as with most people who appeared on the show, they developed a mutual understanding and respect.

The episode of the series that had the highest viewing figures featured two business executives called Charles Bruneau and Gloria Greenleaf. Bruneau was thirty-one and was described by many of his colleagues, both male and female, as a sexist and a misogynist, and some of his ex-girlfriends had described him as *a hedonistic sociopath*.

Gloria Greenleaf was forty-four, a lesbian, and a feminist.

Before swapping jobs, Bruneau was disguised as a woman and Greenleaf was disguised as a man. As, generally speaking, men age better than women, when Bruneau was disguised as a woman, he appeared to be ten years older than he actually was, and when Greenleaf was disguised as a man, she appeared to be ten years younger than her true age.

Bruneau said at the conclusion of his participation in the show, that the nuts and bolts of sexual harassment had been explained to him on numerous occasions by many people but he could never understand what they were talking about, but after six weeks of playing a woman, with his male colleagues leering at his false breasts, touching his false buttocks, invading his personal space, and making condescending remarks whenever they spoke to him, the realities of sexual harassment had been made clear to him.

Greenleaf said at her final interview that, as she had predicted, her subordinate male colleagues were a lot less resentful of her authority when they thought she was a man and her male peers had a lot more respect for her opinions. But she also reported that she was shocked at how blatantly many of her female colleagues had flirted with her.

The episode that Bruneau and Greenleaf had appeared in was especially well-known to Blackmoor as he had included it in a sex education course he had formulated. A very exclusive private mixed sex school had consulted Blackmoor in his capacity as a psychologist because they were experiencing an alarming number of sexual harassment accusations. After reading the reports of the allegations and interviewing the boys and the girls involved, Blackmoor's advice to the school principal commenced with a saying by Robert J. Hanlon: *Never attribute to malice that which is adequately explained by stupidity.* Blackmoor explained that most of the boys were learning about sex from each other, which was largely the blind leading the blind, and a comprehensive sex education course that gave the students the knowledge to make appropriate and healthy choices in their sex lives would solve the problem. The school had been employing an abstinence-only policy, but in response to Blackmoor's recommendations, the principal had engaged Blackmoor to introduce Sex Ed. to his school. Blackmoor designed a comprehensive sex education course, which included the mechanics of procreation, the age of consent, courtship, contraception, safe sex, and, as Blackmoor had often noticed that explaining sexual harassment to boys, or men, was like trying to explain colours to a blind person, he included Bruneau's experiences as a man living as a woman to help clarify the principles of sexual harassment for the boys, as it had done for Bruneau.

The comprehensive sex education course formulated by Blackmoor proved to be so effective that it was adopted by schools, colleges, and universities all over the world.

Blackmoor smiled politely at Jack's witticism that he and a serial killer should go on *A Mile in His Moccasins,* but he'd lost count of the number of times he'd already heard the joke and he no longer found it funny.

"I've also read your book: *If It Makes Sense to You,*" Jack said.

Blackmoor had written a beginner's guide to psychology and it became essential reading for teachers, police officers, nurses, social workers, and anyone else who work with people and require a basic understanding of human behaviour. Blackmoor had named his book *If It Makes Sense to You* to emphasise the need to understand other people's behaviours no matter how bizarre or illogical they appear. To illustrate his point, Blackmoor invited the reader to look introspectively and suggested the reader probably has a phobia, a fetish, or a hobby that makes little or no sense to the vast majority of other people. To further clarify his point, he added that a terror of mice is a common irrational fear but is beyond the comprehension of anyone who doesn't have the phobia. Bondage is a common fetish but getting a thrill from being tied up or tying someone else up is an enigma to anyone who doesn't have the fetish. And that collecting is the most common of all hobbies, but whatever the collector has a penchant for, no matter if it's stamps, foreign coins, or sports memorabilia, the hobby is a mystery to anyone who doesn't have the same passion.

"I have a gambling addiction," Jack said. "I'm no stranger to alcohol, heroin, and cocaine, but gambling is the most irresistible of them all and most people are completely unable to understand that. I explained that the bigger the stake and the longer the odds, the greater the thrill, but my family and friends just kept telling me to pull myself together."

His gambling addiction explains why Jack is competent but homeless, Blackmoor thought to himself.

"I worked as a bookkeeper for an antique dealer, and after my bank refused to loan me any more money, I embezzled money from my employer to feed my gambling habit," Jack continued. "And when I'd lost that, I borrowed from some loan sharks and entered a high-stakes poker tournament. I knew that if I won the tournament, I could pay back the loan sharks and replace the money I'd taken from my employer without him ever knowing I'd taken it. And if I lost the tournament, I'd spend a few years in prison if the loan sharks didn't kill me first."

Blackmoor could see that Jack was getting excited by telling the story and reliving the experience.

"And that poker tournament was the thrill of a lifetime," Jack said. "And I was on a roll to start with. I made it to the final table with just three other players before my luck ran out and I lost everything. And I've been on the run, homeless, and using a false name ever since. But before I went on the run, I sent an email to my ex-wife which said I was going to the Florida everglades to feed myself to the alligators."

As Blackmoor was a psychiatrist, he was accustomed to people telling him their most intimate secrets, and since television had made him famous, people he hardly knew would confide in him, but he was surprised that Jack went as far as to confess to being a felon on the run.

"In your book, you mentioned you've worked with paedophiles, addicts, anorexics, and a variety of other people who wrestle with their own personal demons every single day," Jack said. "And you stated that a psychotherapist needs to have a non-judgmental attitude, unconditional positive regard, and empathy. And I think you've mastered a non-judgemental attitude and unconditional positive regard magnificently, but you can't possibly have any empathy or understanding of people who wrestle with their own personal demons, as you have no demons of your own."

How little you know, Blackmoor thought to himself.

Chapter Seven

Angela Kincaid was a wrestler, a model, and a dominatrix. She was extremely attractive, over six feet tall, and a big-boned amazon with long raven black hair. When she had started her wrestling career, she had called herself *The Banshee*, a tribute to her Irish heritage, but a wrestling commentator had referred to her as *The Kinky Angel*, a play on her name, and the nickname had stuck. She decided to call herself *The Kinky Angel* and she dressed like a leather-clad dominatrix when she wrestled.

As a result of her wrestling demeanour, a firm that manufactured bondage, domination, and sadomasochistic equipment, had asked Angela to model some of their merchandise and she became better known as a BDSM model than as a wrestler.

Then Angela was approached by a film producer who made BDSM films and he offered her the role of a dominatrix. She had accepted his offer and had viewed several of the films he'd produced, as well as several BDSM and fetish films produced by other people, as she wanted to get an idea of what was expected of her. Angela had already had a few small parts on television and she noticed that in stark contrast to television, where a lot of time and trouble is taken over minor details, in the erotic film industry, the scripts were ludicrous, the acting was laughable, and the production emphasis seemed to be on completing the films as quickly and cheaply as possible.

The director of Angela's debut film was a man called Ted Barker, who had directed a great many BDSM films and was a seasoned veteran of the genre. His hallmark was to film a beating from five different directions simultaneously (and he expected his actresses to endure a genuine thrashing) and he would then cut and splice the recordings to make the beating appear to have gone on for five times longer than it actually did. He would also include close-ups, slow-motion replays, and split screen shots if he thought they would improve the film's saleability. Angela was cast as the dominatrix and an actress called Sasha Leigh was cast as the blonde submissive. Sasha was a classically trained actress but had started making sex films when she was unable to get more traditional acting gigs.

Angela was given the screenplay of the film she was to star in and the storyline was Angela kidnaps and disciplines Sasha, who is initially defiant but is disciplined until she is totally subservient. As soon as Angela had read the short script, she said it didn't make sense and she wanted to rewrite it. Ted explained the reason sex and fetish films do not have elaborate plots is most of the people who pay to see them use them as masturbatory aids and generally fast-forward through the non-sex scenes. He added that the films have to be made within a very tight budget and if they cost too much to make, they won't turn a profit. But, despite protests and appeals from Ted, Angela wouldn't acquiesce and Ted had to phone the producer and tell him Angela insisted on rewriting the screenplay. The producer reluctantly agreed as he wanted *The Kinky Angel* to star in one of his films, and Angela, Ted, Sasha, and Ted's film crew wrote a new script.

Angela suggested she could play a sales assistant in a sex shop, which would explain why she was dressed like a dominatrix (thigh boots and a leather basque), and Sasha could play a rich arrogant customer who came into her shop to buy some sex toys. Then Angela recognises Sasha from their college days and remembers Sasha was the president of a sorority that she had tried to join and Sasha had brutally hazed her and a few other pledges with BDSM games. Most of the pledges had dropped out but Angela had toughed out *Hell Week* but still wasn't allowed to join the sorority. Angela later learnt that Sasha had no intention of letting any of the pledges join the sorority and just enjoyed beating and humiliating young girls. Angela would then remind Sasha of where they had met and of what Sasha had done to her, and, after a detailed tirade, she'd drag Sasha to an S&M dungeon to exact sweet revenge.

Angela explained to Ted that this would make the storyline more believable and would make the dominatrix more sympathetic to the audience.

Surprisingly, once Ted and Sasha had focused their attention on making a better film, it brought out the artist in Ted and the actress in Sasha, and they both made suggestions that would improve the script as well as insisting on extensive rehearsals and numerous retakes.

Ted said if they were going to have a long background story in which Angela explains who she was and where they had previously met, they'd have to give the characters names. After quite a lot of debate, they agreed to call the character Sasha was playing *Jade Carrington,* and the character Angela was playing *Bethany McGuinness.*

To make the film look more realistic, Ted shot the first scene in an actual sex shop, and once *Bethany* had dragged *Jade* through a doorway at the back of the establishment, they relocated to an S&M dungeon and Ted cut the film to make it look as if the sex shop and the S&M dungeon were in adjoining rooms.

Bethany commenced the punishment by putting *Jade* across her knees and giving her a hand spanking over the seat of her skirt, which didn't look unfeasible as *Bethany* was a lot bigger and a lot stronger than *Jade.* After the over-the-knee spanking, *Bethany* forced *Jade* to strip naked and fettered her to various pieces of bondage apparatus in the S&M dungeon and beat her with a paddle, a martinet, and ultimately a cane.

At the conclusion of the film, *Bethany* made *Jade* promise to come back and be her maid for a week to make up for the *Hell Week Jade* had made her endure but assured her if she worked hard and was punctual, there'd be no more beatings. *Jade* agreed to this but to ensure her cooperation, *Bethany* fettered *Jade* to a bondage rack and masturbated her with a vibrator until she'd climaxed. *Bethany* then told *Jade* she'd video-recorded her climaxing, and if she went to the police, *Bethany* would show them the video recording and claim *Jade* had paid to be dominated, and if *Jade* didn't return to work as her maid, she'd put the video recording on the internet.

During the filming, Angela had to play anger, vengeful gratification, and mild sexual arousal, but Sasha had to play arrogance, outrage, terror, and pain, and had to fake an orgasm, and it was extremely fortunate she was a skilled and talented classically trained actress.

They called the film *Payback's a Bitch* and it took over two weeks to make, whereas it was expected to be filmed in a day. The producer had said it had cost so much to make that it wouldn't turn a profit, but he was very wrong. It was a smash hit in the BDSM scene and because of the subject matter and the realism, there was no end of protests about the film, and the consequent controversy and publicity made certain that even people who didn't normally watch sex or BDSM films wanted to see it.

The film kickstarted Sasha's acting career and she was offered a major role in a TV series.

Angela and Ted continued to make BDSM films, with an emphasis on realistic storylines, and the next film they made together was called *The Parole Officer*. Angela played the titular role and it was explained at the beginning of the film that she had a very impressive track record and the female parolees in her care seldom reoffended or violated their parole. On the rare occasions one of them did so, Angela would give her the option of returning to prison or accepting corporal punishment. The severity of the punishment would depend on the seriousness of the violation and how many times she had already violated her parole.

In total, Angela and Ted made fifty-five films together, and although Ted continued to employ girls who had glamour model good looks, he would occasionally hire women who were middle-aged, overweight, and homely to add realism to his films. The most successful and controversial of all the films they had made together were the *Surprise Bondage Tickle Torture* series. The plot of the series of films was Ted had employed women for the sole purpose

The Spectre

of modelling fetish outfits and bondage equipment and once they were restrained and helpless, Angela would tickle them mercilessly and apparently without their permission or prior knowledge. For realism, Ted had only used actresses who were genuinely ticklish, and most of the people who saw the films honestly believed that the women were being tickled without their consent. Ted received numerous emails protesting the ill-treatment of his models and a few people even reported the abuse of the women to the police, but before shooting the films, Ted had video recorded his actresses stating they were aware they were going to be tickled and were able to stop the filming at any time they chose, and Ted emailed the video recordings to anyone who expressed concern.

Ted considered making some films in which the fettered women were spanked, paddled, and caned with the pretence it was being done without their prior knowledge or consent but he thought that might be too much realism.

As a consequence of her BDSM film career, Angela lost count of the number of exorbitant offers she had received to dominate men, women, and couples, and eventually she became a licensed sex worker and trained to be a dominatrix: because of the number of injuries suffered by people who were dominated by sex workers who were unfamiliar with BDSM, before a sex worker could work as a dominatrix, she had to have special training.

Angela continued to wrestle, and her partner for mixed-sex tag team matches was a man called Forest "The Invincible" Hightower, who was even more famous than she was.

Forest Hightower was six feet eight inches tall, broad-shouldered, and heavily muscled. He became a household name in 2123 when he'd won the Olympic gold medals for both Greco-Roman and freestyle wrestling in the super heavyweight divisions.

The 2123 Athens Olympic Wrestling Tournament had received an unprecedented amount of media attention because it had been a trial event for some new innovations in the Olympic Games: many Olympic officials had noted that staging the numerous events that take place at the Olympic Games was an administrative nightmare and it was suggested that some of the events could be held at a different time and place to the rest of the Games to ease the organisational pressure and the wrestling events were selected to be held separately, although they would still have the prestige of the Olympic Games.

Partly because wrestling was one of the events that were held at the ancient Greek Olympic Games, Athens was chosen to be the permanent location of the Olympic wrestling events, unlike all the other events, which would continue to be held at a different city every four years. The Athenians had built an indoor stadium especially to be the home of Olympic wrestling and had borrowed much of the architecture and décor from the ancient Greeks and had tributes to their gods, their heroes, and their Olympic Games all over the stadium in the forms of statues, mosaics, and wall carvings.

Hightower became a professional wrestler shortly after the 2123 Athens Olympic Wrestling Tournament and he currently had the largest fan following of any wrestler in the world.

As he had never lost a wrestling match as either an Olympian or a professional, a sports journalist referred to him as Forest "The Invincible" Hightower and it became his epithet.

Forest Hightower had briefly crossed paths with Dr. Dominic Blackmoor in 2130: Blackmoor was a world-renowned forensic psychiatrist but was equally as renowned as a psychologist and a government anti-smoking committee had approached him and had asked him how they could stop the people of America smoking. They said tobacco companies had been banned from advertising or displaying their products, the sale of cigarettes had been restricted, smoking had been banned in many public places, and billions of dollars had been spent on anti-smoking campaigns, but millions of Americans were still smoking.

Blackmoor submitted a report that said their main approach had been to encourage people to give up smoking once they were already addicted to nicotine, but a better approach would be to prevent children, adolescents, and young adults from becoming addicted in the first place. He acknowledged that documentary films that graphically outlined the dangers of smoking had been recurrently shown in schools but had had little effect because they were basically adults telling children not to smoke, and the most counterproductive thing an adult can say to a child or to an adolescent is *Don't do as I do, do as I say!*

Blackmoor recommended that the anti-smoking documentaries continue to be shown in schools but suggested they include celebrities (role models) stating they don't smoke as the best way to motivate a child or young adult is to lead by example. Blackmoor added it was crucial that the celebs honestly don't smoke, as children and teenagers don't like being lied to. Many superstars were approached, including Forest Hightower, and the vast majority of them agreed to appear for free. Within three months of the film being shown in schools, cigarette manufacturers reported a very minor reduction in sales and every quarter the sale of cigarettes continued to decline as the youth of America imitated their heroes and role models and didn't take up the habit of smoking. It was predicted that if the trend continued, within thirty years, cigarettes would be as uncommon as snuff.

Several surveys indicated that of all the celebrities who had appeared in the anti-smoking documentaries, Forest Hightower had had the most influence on the youth of America.

Hightower had recently ventured into acting and had played Frankenstein's monster in a film. The director's interpretation of the monster had been based on Mary Shelley's descriptions:

Oh! No mortal could support the horror of that countenance. A mummy again endued with animation could not be so hideous as the demoniacal corpse to which I had so miserably given life. I had gazed on him while unfinished; he was ugly then, but when those muscles and joints were rendered capable of motion, it became a thing such as even Dante could not have conceived.

Its unearthly ugliness rendered it almost too horrible for human eyes.

The monster was the shape of a man but of gigantic stature, about eight feet in height, and distorted in its proportions.

Great God! His yellow skin scarcely covered the work of muscles and arteries beneath; his hair was of a lustrous black and flowing; his teeth of a pearly whiteness; but these luxuriances only formed a more horrid contrast with his watery eyes, that seemed almost of the same colour as the dun white sockets in which they were set, his shrivelled complexion and straight black lips.

When casting all the other parts in the film, the director had only chosen actors and actresses who were no taller than four feet eleven inches, and, as Hightower was six feet eight inches tall, by comparison, Hightower appeared to be about eight feet in height. As well as the height, Hightower had bulging muscles like a bodybuilder, and the makeup artists who made him look scarred and ugly had little trouble making Hightower look as if he'd been stitched together in a laboratory.

As Forest Hightower was considered to be one of the toughest men in the world and Angela Kincaid was considered to be one of the sexiest women in the world, *The Spectre* had had them in mind since the beginning of his campaign of terror. He studied their routines but had trouble finding the right time and place to engage them as, although they wrestled as a tag team, they had separate careers that kept them apart for much of the time. But *The Spectre* had learnt that whenever they had a gig in Los Angeles, they'd often meet at a bordello called *Cats & Kittens* that had a large S&M dungeon, where Angela worked as a dominatrix. The *Cats & Kittens* S&M dungeon was well equipped with a lot of elaborate bondage apparatus and numerous sex toys, and Angela had shot several BDSM films there.

It was Sunday morning and Hightower was driving to the bordello to pick up Angela as they were going to make an appearance at a charity event to help raise money for the Third World. She had been working as a dominatrix on Saturday night and, as she frequently did when she had worked late, spent the night at *Cats & Kittens*.

When Hightower arrived at the bordello, he was surprised to see the "CLOSED" sign was on display and the main gates were shut. Although Sunday mornings were the slackest times of the week, *Cats & Kittens* was usually open for business twenty-four hours a day, seven days a week.

"This is Hightower. I've come to pick up Angela," he said into the intercom at the main gates.

The electronically controlled gates swung open, Hightower drove in, and the gates closed behind him. He parked his car, entered the bordello via the front door, and was confronted by a man pointing a pistol at him.

"Take out your smartphone and place it on the desk," the gunman instructed.

Hightower complied and the gunman then ordered him to walk to the S&M dungeon.

As they walked through the bordello, they passed the dead bodies of several security guards, sex workers, and customers who'd been shot to death.

Hightower entered the S&M dungeon and saw Angela and another three girls: Heidi, Gloria, and Buffy. They were all still alive and uninjured but had been gagged and fettered. *The Spectre* had cherry-picked the four most beautiful sex workers in the bordello and had allowed them to live for a little longer so he could use them for his own amusement.

Then Hightower noticed that some words had been written on the wall with Angel's lipstick:

"BE AFRAID!

BE VERY AFRAID!"

Sometimes Angela wore cherry red lipstick and at other times wore jet black lipstick and the gunman had held both tubes of lipstick in one hand when he'd written the words and the jet black shadowed the cherry red. When Hightower saw the words, he realised the gunman was the serial killer the police and the media had named *The Spectre* and knew he'd soon be fighting for his life, as well as the lives of Angela and the other three girls.

As Hightower turned to face his adversary, *The Spectre* removed the ammunition clip from his pistol and placed the gun on the floor.

"Mano a mano," *The Spectre* said.

Hightower lunged at *The Spectre* with the intention of dragging his smaller opponent to the floor and overpower him with his colossal weight advantage. *The Spectre* evaded the giant's charge, seized his arm, and threw him to the floor with a ju-jitsu technique. Hightower landed heavily on his back, and the room shook like a minor earthquake, but he knew how to break a fall and quickly regained his footing. He again lunged at *The Spectre,* and again *The Spectre* threw him to the floor.

It was obvious to Hightower that *The Spectre* was toying with him like a cat playing with a mouse and he knew he'd have to change his strategy. He circled *The Spectre*, and when he saw his chance, he attacked, but he didn't employ a wrestling technique, which he thought *The Spectre* would be expecting, instead he attacked with a punch to *The Spectre's* face. *The Spectre* dodged Hightower's haymaker and then swept his legs out from under him with a sweeping kick.

Although *The Spectre* was using ju-jitsu techniques, his style of combat resembled a bullfighter more than a ju-jitsu master.

The Spectre gave Hightower time to recover and out of desperation and frustration, Hightower charged *The Spectre* like a linebacker. *The Spectre* responded with a kick to Hightower's chest but it was like kicking a charging rhino and the force of the impact sent *The Spectre* tumbling backwards. *The Spectre* rolled once and finished in a crouching position, and as Hightower leapt towards him,

The Spectre sprang up and kicked Hightower in the face, knocking him out cold.

When Hightower regained consciousness, he was sitting in a chair. He had a throbbing pain across the left side of his face and his cheekbone had been fractured. Hightower could taste blood and explored the inside of his mouth with his tongue and the upper teeth on the left side of his mouth had been knocked out. He opened his eyes and his left eye was badly swollen and closing up. Hightower tried to get up but his hands were manacled behind his back and there was a leather belt around his neck. As he struggled against the restraints, his head started to clear and he remembered the fight he'd had with *The Spectre* and realised that his hands had been cuffed behind his back and the leather belt around his neck had been threaded through some cupboard door handles: he'd seen news reports of how *The Spectre* operated and he could feel the cupboard door handles against the back of his neck.

As his head cleared, he looked around the room and saw Angela and the other three girls were naked and fettered to different bondage machines. Gloria was strapped face forward to a bondage cross, Heidi was bent over a punishment trestle with her wrists and ankles strapped down, and Buffy had been manacled face down on a bondage rack. Angela was suspended by her wrists with her feet about twelve inches off the floor but her legs were not tied together.

The Spectre was sorting through the spanking paddles, canes, martinets, tawses, leather straps, riding crops, and whips that were in abundance at the *Cats & Kittens* S&M dungeon. He selected a paddle that was about the size of a table tennis bat and then looked around at the girls. He already knew which girl he was going to start with but he took some time pretending to decide to keep the girls in terrified suspense.

Eventually, *The Spectre* went to Gloria who was strapped face forward to a bondage cross and gave her a hard whack across her butt. The deathly silence was suddenly broken by the loud smack of the paddle against Gloria's bottom and the muffled cries of the four girls as they all tried to scream with ball gags strapped in their mouths. Gloria tensed every muscle in her body as a result of the stinging pain and then gradually relaxed as the sting faded. As soon as she had unclenched her buttocks, *The Spectre* whacked her again. After about half a dozen whacks, Gloria realised that *The Spectre* was getting off on watching her react to the pain and she tried to lay still. She endured about sixty whacks and could force herself not to tense her muscles or to cry out but she couldn't stop the tears from running down her face or the fair skin on her butt cheeks from turning red.

Then *The Spectre* moved on to Buffy, who was manacled face down on a bondage rack. He chose to beat her with a very flexible cane and made several practice swings as the swishing sound the cane made as it cut through the air frightened the girls. He then ran the cane slowly and gently across Buffy's pert backside, and he even let the cane gently drop and bounce off the muscular firmness of her buttocks a few times. Then he raised the cane and gave her a hard stroke across the meatiest part of her bottom. Buffy tried not to react to the pain, and this wasn't the first time she'd been caned, but she'd been paid thousands of dollars for every other caning she'd received. *The Spectre* waited for the red welt to appear across her backside, before giving her another stroke. After about thirty strokes, Buffy's bottom was crisscrossed with red stripes, and he shifted his attention to Angela.

Angela was suspended by her wrists and *The Spectre* decided to thrash her with the same whippy cane he'd used on Buffy. He gave Angela a hard stroke across her buttocks and she bent her arms, kicked her legs, and bobbed up and down like a string puppet. She tried to shout threats and abuse at *The Spectre* but the ball gag that had been strapped into her mouth made most of what she said unintelligible. *The Spectre* gave her about sixty strokes of the cane and towards the end of the beating, she'd stopped struggling and just groaned after every stroke.

The Spectre

Then *The Spectre* moved onto Heidi, who was bent over a punishment trestle. He chose to flog her with a martinet and started to lash her butt.

Hightower had lost count of the number of times he'd tried with all his might to break the handcuffs but even after he'd lost all hope of doing so, he continued to flex his muscles against the handcuffs out of anguish and frustration as he helplessly watched the girls being tortured. Then suddenly, and much to his surprise, one of the cuffs popped open and his hands were free. Hightower stealthily kept his hands behind his back while he planned his next move. First, he'd have to break the leather belt that was around his neck and he tensed his neck muscles and leaned forwards with all his strength. Initially, the leather belt wouldn't budge, but Hightower kept tensing and relaxing his muscles. Gradually, there was more and more slack in the belt as the cupboard door handles that the belt had been threaded through were little by little breaking away from the cupboard doors. Then one of the handles broke away from the door and Hightower knew that once he'd pulled off the other handle, he'd be free to take action.

The Spectre was walking in circles around Heidi to whip her from different directions, and just as the second handle broke away from the door, *The Spectre* was standing about ten feet away from Hightower, with his back to him. Hightower rushed *The Spectre*, put him in a stranglehold, and started to choke him.

The Spectre pulled at the enormous forearm that was choking him and kicked with both legs like a man being hanged as his larger opponent had lifted him clear of the floor. It took a few moments for *The Spectre* to overcome the initial shock and switch from his basic animal instincts to his martial arts training. *The Spectre* pulled on Hightower's wrist with his left hand and elbowed him in the midsection with his right arm. Hightower's grip loosened enough for *The Spectre* to slip out of the stranglehold, and as he turned to face the giant, Hightower locked him in a bear hug. *The Spectre* wheezed as his ribs were compressed and he pushed frantically on Hightower's head to escape his deadly embrace and snatch a quick breath before he lost consciousness. Using his last reserves of oxygen, *The Spectre* seized the hair on the back of Hightower's head with his left hand, grabbed Hightower's chin with his right hand, and twisted the giant's head with all his strength and speed. Hightower's neck snapped and they both fell limply to the floor. *The Spectre* was gasping for breath and Hightower's arms and legs were twitching. Hightower was probably dead but *The Spectre* hoped he was alive but paralysed from the neck down and would be fully aware of everything that was going to happen to the four girls.

"At last," *The Spectre* said to Hightower as soon as he'd got his breath back. "A worthy opponent; it's a pity we can only do this once."

Chapter Eight

Blackmoor enthusiastically watched all the morning news reports about *The Spectre's* latest murders at the *Cats & Kittens* bordello, and he wanted to use his law enforcement connections to learn more, but he had an appointment to see a new patient.

Although Blackmoor had specialized in forensic psychiatry, he continued to treat non-forensic patients and had an appointment to see a man called George Claridge, who was a billionaire from a well-to-do family. Claridge's father had brought him into the family business and he had proved himself to be such a proficient businessman that his father had retired and placed him in charge of the family business empire.

On the death of his father, Claridge had converted all the family assets into investments, enabling him to make enormous profits by doing very little work, and he spent the time he'd freed up by indulging in his obsession: *necrophilia: a sexual attraction to dead bodies.*

Claridge became a funeral director and trained to be a mortuary cosmetologist, and if an attractive female corpse was sent to his funeral home, he'd return to the mortuary late at night when all his staff had gone home and had sexual intercourse with her dead body. He did this on numerous occasions until the body of a particularly attractive twenty-two-year-old girl came to his funeral home. After placing her naked body on a table and beautifying her, he disrobed and had sexual intercourse with her.

Before Claridge returned her body to the refrigerator, he took some photographs of her, which he routinely did with all the corpses he'd had sexual intercourse with to enable him to recall the experience at a later time.

Claridge then saw her eyes were open and staring at him. He thought perhaps her eyelids had popped open, as happens with some cadavers, but as he walked around the table, her sapphire blue eyes followed him.

Claridge realised she must have been in a coma. He thought through his options and reasoned that as she'd already been certified as dead and scheduled for an unattended cremation, if he killed her, he'd never be caught. Claridge took a cushion from one of the coffins with the intention of pressing it onto her nose and mouth and suffocating her. He sat astride her abdomen with the cushion in his hands for several minutes before he accepted the fact that he couldn't go through with it and phoned for an ambulance.

Claridge hoped she wouldn't remember what he'd done to her but within an hour the girl had recovered sufficiently from her coma to report she'd been raped. As part of their investigation, the police searched Claridge's apartment and found photographs of forty-six female corpses, and when questioned, he admitted that he'd had sexual intercourse with each and every one of them. Claridge was prosecuted but he could afford the very best legal representation money could buy and the judge agreed to a suspended sentence.

Claridge then relocated from Boston to Los Angeles and tried to start a new life.

Claridge had made an appointment to see Blackmoor, although seeing a psychiatrist wasn't one of the conditions of his suspended sentence, and after a brief introduction, they began their first session.

"How can I help you?" Blackmoor asked.

"Did you read the reports I gave to your personal assistant?" Claridge responded. He'd given Blackmoor's personal assistant a précis of the transcripts of his court case and a short single-page autobiography.

"Yes, I read them," Blackmoor said.

"You're aware I've had sexual intercourse with dead bodies but I don't disgust you," Claridge said with some surprise. "When the police had learnt what I'd done, they were appalled by me. My own lawyers, who I paid a fortune to defend me, were horrified and sickened by me. And in the process of working as a funeral director, I established friendships with clergymen of every denomination, and even they thought I was beyond redemption. But I don't disgust you."

"I'm not a policeman, a lawyer, or a clergyman," Blackmoor replied. "I'm a doctor."

Claridge seemed impressed by Blackmoor's answer and started to talk about his problems: "My fetish with death started when I was eleven. I'm from old money and my family resided in a large mansion house with a great many live-in servants, including one particularly attractive maid called Christiana. I had an incredible crush on her and I'd follow her around the house and watch her while she worked. Then her fiancé broke off their engagement and she committed suicide by taking a bottle of sleeping tablets. Christiana's family had served my family for five generations and my father paid for an elaborate funeral. The undertakers beautified her and laid her out in an open coffin in the great hall of our mansion house, so her family and friends could pay their last respects, and the night before her funeral, I sneaked down to her coffin and put my hands all over her body, and I've been sexually attracted to dead bodies ever since."

Throughout his declaration, Claridge was studying Blackmoor's facial expressions to gauge his emotional responses.

"I controlled my desires with pornography for many years but the thoughts became increasingly persistent and the desires became ever stronger and I decided to become a funeral director to gain access to dead bodies," Claridge continued. "I reasoned I wasn't doing anyone any harm, as the girls were already dead and their relatives would never find out."

Blackmoor identified with Claridge in as much as he too had antisocial drives that he found clandestine ways of controlling: Blackmoor had homicidal urges that he controlled by studying and hunting serial killers, and he had sadistic cravings that he satiated by having sexual relationships with masochistic partners.

"Since relocating to Los Angeles, I've become involved in the Goth fetish scene," Claridge said. "I adopt the persona of a vampire and make love to girls who are also into the scene or to prostitutes who are familiar with the Goth fetish. My favourite lover is a sex worker who calls herself *Countess Dracula*, who has long raven black hair and very fair skin. She's primarily a dominatrix but I pay her to lie completely still and pretend to be a dormant vampire while I make love to her, and I fantasize that she's a corpse."

Blackmoor suspected that Claridge was aware there was no cure for his problem but being able to confide his deepest darkest secrets to someone who was completely non-judgemental would give him some relief.

"I've started to have daydreams about murdering *Countess Dracula*, embalming her dead body, and keeping her as a sex toy," Claridge continued.

Most people, even most psychiatrists, would have been shocked by Claridge's last statement, but Blackmoor had heard a lot worse.

"But I'd never act out my fantasies," Claridge added. "I've read the book you authored, *If It Makes Sense to You*, in which you stated, 'There's nothing wrong with what you think or what you feel, only in what you do.'"

Blackmoor acknowledged he had made the statement and Claridge continued: "If my murderous desires ever became more than I could control, I'd choose suicide before I'd choose homicide."

That's something else we have in common, Blackmoor thought to himself.

Chapter Nine

FBI Supervisory Special Agent Ramona Cortez began her career in law enforcement in the New York Police Department and had worked her way up through the ranks and had attained the much-coveted position of lieutenant in the Homicide Division. While working as a homicide detective for the NYPD, Cortez had investigated a few serial killers and during the investigations had liaised with the criminal profilers of the FBI's Behavioural Analysis Unit.

The FBI's Behavioural Analysis Unit was continuously contacted by local and state law enforcement agencies for assistance with their cases. Frequently the police officers who approached them were inexperienced with homicide investigations and would ask the BAU for help when criminal profiling wasn't the first best course of action and what they really needed was the advice of a seasoned homicide detective. In response to this, the BAU had invited a few exceptional homicide detectives to join their ranks and Ramona Cortez was the first person they had thought of.

As an FBI Supervisory Special Agent, she had advised law enforcement agencies all over America and if a serial killer had offended in more than one state, and the investigation was already under federal jurisdiction, Cortez was the FBI's star homicide detective.

The first case in which she had liaised with Blackmoor was *The Las Vegas Strangler* investigation: in 2126 an attractive female tourist had been murdered in a Las Vegas hotel room. The autopsy revealed she had been stunned with an electroshock weapon to subdue her and had then been rendered unconscious with chloroform repeatedly over at least a six-hour period until she died of a chloroform overdose. The crime scene investigators processed the hotel room and surmised that during the six hours she had been unconscious and for about three hours after she had died, she had been repeatedly repositioned in different parts of the room, probably to be photographed. Her attacker had also changed her clothing and reapplied her makeup several times.

Because of the bizarre nature of the crime, and the fact that the murder victim had been a rich and attractive woman, the case got a lot of attention, and the police and the media were thinking *serial killer* even before the second murder had occurred. The police referred to the killer as *The Las Vegas Strangler* and kept most of his modus operandi a secret, as they correctly predicted they would lose count of the number of false confessions they would receive and if the media and the general public believed the killer murdered with strangulation and not chloroform, they could easily weed out the false confessions.

Five weeks later, an attractive young professional dancer was killed in her own home with the same modus operandi.

The Las Vegas homicide detectives were neither inexperienced nor incompetent, but they could not catch the killer and the murders continued.

To start with, the murders had occurred every four to six weeks, but the seventh and eighth murders had occurred within three days of each other and had led the police to believe they were dealing with two killers: either the killer and a copycat or the killer and his apprentice. Having two serial killers with the same modus operandi in the same place at the same time meant one could kill while the other established an ironclad alibi and vice-versa, which made it impossible to shorten the enormous and ever-growing list of suspects.

After the seventeenth murder, the frustrated Las Vegas homicide detectives had invited FBI Supervisory Special Agent Ramona Cortez to take charge of the investigation. They had already consulted the FBI's criminal profilers but as the body count was now up to seventeen and they were no nearer catching the killer – or killers – they were desperate enough to ask Cortez for help.

Cortez knew of Blackmoor by reputation and shortly after she had taken charge of the investigation, had asked him to profile *The Las Vegas Strangler.*

Blackmoor read the police reports of each of the murders and agreed they were dealing with two killers. He believed the copycat killer had killed four of the women because in only four of the murders had the killer taken trophies from his victims: he'd taken jewellery that the women had been wearing when he had attacked them.

The copycat killer knew so much about *The Las Vegas Strangler's* modus operandi that if he hadn't partnered with him, he must have had access to the closely guarded confidential police investigation files. Blackmoor asked the computer for a list of people who had had access to the files prior to the seventh murder and one name caught his attention: Gerard Deacon, Ph.D. Gerard Deacon was a psychology teacher who had written two books about serial killers (both of which Blackmoor had read) and after the fifth murder had volunteered to profile *The Las Vegas Strangler.* It was Deacon who had first suggested that most of the murders had been committed by a team of two killers and the homicides in which things had been taken from the crime scenes had been carried out solely by the submissive member of the duo. He speculated that the dominant partner only took photographs to re-experience the murders, but once the submissive member of the team had started killing without his dominant partner's supervision, he'd also taken jewellery that the women had been wearing when he had attacked them as the jewellery was of personal significance to his victims and made ideal trophies.

Blackmoor had phoned Deacon and asked him if they could collaborate on the case and Deacon had enthusiastically agreed to a meeting with the famous Dr. Dominic Blackmoor.

They met at the task force headquarters and as well as talking about the case, they talked about the other homicide investigations Blackmoor had taken part in and the books Deacon had written, and the more they talked, the more Blackmoor was convinced that Deacon was the copycat killer.

After their meeting, Blackmoor asked the computer to take the four murders he believed Deacon to be responsible for out of the equation and to reprioritise the list of suspects for the remaining thirteen homicides.

In seconds the computer had displayed a list of names and Blackmoor studied each of the suspects as they occurred on the list.

The third man on the list was a photographer called Raymond Parker. Parker had no criminal record and no obvious way of obtaining chloroform, but he became a suspect when a model had phoned the tip hotline and reported that Parker was notorious for taking pictures of girls while they were sleeping. She added that several girls at her modelling agency had mentioned they'd blacked out at parties, had woken up in their own beds, and had later learnt that Parker had taken them home. As they were not sexually molested, the girls had assumed they'd had too much to drink and he'd escorted them home, but now they were wondering if Parker had drugged them to take pictures of them while they were unconscious.

Parker had been questioned by the police and had said as he worked for one of the biggest advertising agencies in Las Vegas, he'd taken pictures of girls in every conceivable context, and not just while they were sleeping, and if any of his models got drunk at parties, he ensured they got home safely.

As Parker was a renowned photographer, Blackmoor was able to find a colossal amount of information about him on the internet, and after reading about him and viewing many of the pictures he'd taken, Blackmoor believed he was *The Las Vegas Strangler*.

The Spectre

Blackmoor told Cortez he believed Raymond Parker was *The Las Vegas Strangler* and Gerard Deacon was the copycat killer. She responded by saying a judge wouldn't sign arrest or search warrants based on a profiler's sixth sense and the best she could do was to place Parker and Deacon on twenty-four-hour surveillance.

Eight days into the surveillance, the police officers who were shadowing Parker followed him to the home of a model he had previously photographed. As she opened her front door, Parker pulled an electroshock weapon from his satchel, stunned her with it, and carried her back into her house. The surprised policemen were watching Parker at a distance with night vision binoculars and it took them a couple of minutes to run to the house and kick down the front door. On crashing through the door, they caught Parker with a bottle of chloroform in one hand and a chloroform-soaked rag in the other.

Parker's house was searched and thirteen photo albums were found (one for each of his victims), which contained detailed pictorial stories of the slow deaths of the thirteen women he had murdered.

Parker made a full confession and said he had a fetish for watching and photographing girls while they were sleeping and after they were dead.

Five days after Parker's arrest, the police officers conducting the surveillance of Deacon followed him to the motel room of an attractive young lady who was holidaying in Las Vegas. Deacon's attack on the young lady was almost identical to Parker's attack on the model, and Deacon's arrest was almost identical to Parker's arrest.

Deacon's residence was searched and the jewellery that had been taken from four of the victims was discovered and, like Parker, he had kept detailed pictorial stories of the women he had murdered.

When confronted with the evidence, Deacon said he'd had an obsessional fascination with serial killers since childhood but the vast majority of their kills were sadistic, brutal, messy, and ugly, whereas *The Las Vegas Strangler* killed with great elegance and at long last, he'd found a serial killer he could emulate.

When *The Spectre* investigation had been handed to the FBI, it had been allocated to Ramona Cortez, who was currently in Los Angeles as that was the location of the last two crime scenes.

Ramona and Blackmoor had been lovers since their collaboration on *The Las Vegas Strangler* investigation and as she happened to be in Los Angeles, she had arranged another liaison.

They had agreed to meet at her apartment, and as Ramona liked being tied up even more than she liked being spanked, Blackmoor had brought his bondage equipment in a sports bag.

When he arrived, Ramona was wearing a matching bra and panties set with black seamed stockings and a suspender belt. She was also wearing a long bathrobe to conceal her underwear as she felt ridiculous wearing erotic lingerie as she was almost fifty years old, five feet eleven inches tall, and a size twenty, but she knew the get-up excited Blackmoor. Blackmoor had repeatedly told her she was curvaceous and voluptuous but she had always thought of herself as being fat.

Ramona asked Blackmoor if he wanted a beverage and when he politely declined her offer, she led him into her bedroom. Once there, she stepped out of her slippers and dropped her bathrobe to the floor, and, after positioning two pillows in the centre of the bed, laid face down on the bed with the pillows under her hips to elevate her bottom.

Blackmoor undressed and then secured her wrists and ankles to the bedposts in a spread-eagle position. He used padded leather manacles, and not ropes or handcuffs, as it excited him to watch his submissive partners struggle – and it generally excited his partners to struggle against the restraints – and metal handcuffs cut into the skin and ropes burnt. Leather manacles were also a lot faster to apply than ropes and unless one of his submissive partners had a penchant for ropes or metal handcuffs, Blackmoor would routinely use padded leather manacles.

Once the bondage was complete, Blackmoor started to give Ramona a massage. He changed the massage from hard, soft, and tickly in an unpredictable pattern, as he knew from previous experience that was what she liked.

Then suddenly, he grabbed her left ankle and started to tickle her foot. Ramona was very ticklish and she laughed uncontrollably and struggled frantically against the restraints but didn't say the safe word as she enjoyed being tickled; she especially enjoyed being tickled while being restrained as struggling against the bondage fetters made her feel truly overpowered and dominated.

After several minutes of tickling her feet, sides, and armpits, Blackmoor started gently patting her bottom on alternate butt cheeks and teasing her with a mock spanking. At sporadic intervals, Blackmoor would stop patting her bottom and would stroke, massage, tickle, and gently grasp handfuls of her ample butt.

After about a hundred love pats, he picked up one of her carpet slippers and placed it on her buttocks. Ramona enjoyed the indignity of being spanked with her own slipper and of having it placed on her butt until Blackmoor was ready to beat her with it.

He then started to massage and stroke her legs and feet as he liked the feel of her stockings.

When he was ready, he picked up the slipper, kissed her on both butt cheeks, and started to whack her bottom, although there wasn't much force behind the whacks as she enjoyed the domination more than the pain.

During their previous liaisons, Blackmoor had given Ramona mock thrashings with several sex toys, including paddles, martinets, straps, riding crops, and canes, but the slipper was her favourite toy.

As this was the climax of the spanking, Blackmoor intended to beat Ramona until she asked him to stop. He didn't mind how long it went on for, as it thrilled him to watch her ample backside ripple after every whack of the slipper while she kept still with her eyes closed and a smile on her face.

"Take me now," she eventually said.

Blackmoor unbuckled the manacles that were securing her ankles and pulled off her panties before freeing her hands. Ramona rolled onto her back and Blackmoor kissed her passionately on the mouth while petting her generous breasts and moist vagina. After a time, Blackmoor put on a condom and mounted Ramona, and she climaxed twice before Blackmoor had finished.

Chapter Ten

While working at his office, Blackmoor saw a patient every hour on the hour, and his 2 pm appointment was with a police officer called Harry Logan. Logan had been involved in a very traumatic gun battle and it was mandatory that he had a minimum of six counselling sessions and be certified as fit by a police psychiatrist before he could return to active duty.

Logan was in the Internal Affairs Bureau and had been investigating two police officers called Donald Kelly and Pancho Guerrero, who had been taking bribes from the *coyotes*: *coyotes* were criminals who illegally smuggled people into the USA for a fee or to use as slave labour. As well as taking bribes from the *coyotes*, Kelly and Guerrero had also been extorting money and sexual favours from the illegal immigrants. Faced with the possibility of losing their jobs, their pensions, and going to prison, Kelly and Guerrero had ambushed Logan and his partner with the intention of shooting them to death. Logan's partner was killed in the initial volley, and in the subsequent shoot-out, Logan was wounded twice before he shot dead both corrupt policemen.

Blackmoor's personal assistant escorted Logan into Blackmoor's office, and once they were seated in armchairs, Blackmoor began their first session.

"Unless you tell me you're going to harm yourself or someone else, everything you say to me will be completely confidential," Blackmoor said.

"As you've probably learnt from my personnel file, I've already been involved in a few shooting incidents," Logan replied. "And on every occasion, it was compulsory that I see a police psychiatrist, so I'm familiar with the protocol."

Logan was in his late fifties and during his long and colourful police career had had to use his gun on numerous occasions.

"Your partner was killed while he was on duty with you, you were shot twice and you may have been killed or disabled, and you shot and killed two men," Blackmoor said. "Of all of these, which caused you the most distress?"

"It was five months ago and I've completely recovered from it physically and emotionally," Logan replied. His strategy was to say whatever he believed would convince Blackmoor to certify him as fit to return to active duty, even if there was no truth in it whatsoever. Blackmoor had anticipated this and knew he'd have to establish a rapport with Logan before Logan would be completely frank and honest with him.

"Being a policeman is probably the most stressful job imaginable," Blackmoor said. "You're involved in gun battles that would give a Navy SEAL nightmares, you see injuries that would make a combat medic throw up, you hear confessions that would make a Catholic priest lose faith, and you have to make choices between the lesser and the greater evil that would make the director of the CIA lose sleep."

"So, you've been around cops long enough to appreciate that," Logan replied rhetorically and with some surprise. "You asked me what the worst part of the shooting was," he continued after a thoughtful pause. "It's being a forgotten hero."

"A forgotten hero?" Blackmoor said with a questioning tone of voice, enabling Logan to expand on his statement. Instead of asking questions, repeating back something a patient had just said but repeating it in a questioning tone of voice was a counselling technique Blackmoor frequently employed.

"Quite a few years ago, when I was a patrolman, I was involved in a similar shooting incident," Logan continued. "I was partnered with a rookie and we were sent to investigate reports of screaming coming from a house in an affluent Beverly Hills neighbourhood.

The Spectre

When we arrived at the house it was completely silent. I rang the doorbell, repeatedly, and eventually the occupants responded by shooting at us through the closed door. My partner was shot but not killed and we both ducked for cover and called for backup. I later learnt it was a team of four gunmen from Louisiana."

Blackmoor was very familiar with the gun battle and even remembered hearing about it on the news when he was a boy. Even as a boy, Blackmoor had a fascination for serial killers and read everything he could find on the internet about the four Louisiana gunmen. They'd carried out a number of home invasions in Louisiana, in which they'd stolen cash and valuables and murdered all the people they'd robbed to eliminate any witnesses. In some of the home invasions, young women had been abducted and never seen again. Louisiana law enforcement officers had surmised the young women had been raped and murdered at a later time and place and their bodies had been disposed of, probably by throwing them to the alligators in the Louisiana swamps. Also, an alarming number of people were mysteriously going missing, tourists as well as members of the indigenous population, and some investigators had suspected they were being abducted and murdered by the same team who were conducting the home invasions.

Perhaps the four gunmen thought the Louisiana police were closing in on them, or perhaps they wanted to prey on a more moneyed community where their home invasions would yield larger profits, but for whatever reason, they decided to relocate to Los Angeles. The first thing they did on reaching LA was a home invasion in Beverly Hills, where they found a married couple and their two young children. They bound and gagged the mother and her children and then forced the husband and father to tell them where he kept his cash and any other valuables. Once they'd collected everything worth stealing and were ready to leave, the leader of the gang told his three cohorts to kill the man and his two children but not to kill the woman as they were taking her with them. One of the gunmen drew a large Bowie knife and was just about to start slaughtering the children and their father, when Logan rang the front doorbell.

"In the shoot-out, and before backup arrived, I shot dead three of the gunmen before I was wounded, and I shot and killed the last one after I was wounded," Logan continued.

Blackmoor remembered reading that stolen property in possession of the four gunmen was traced back to five home invasions, eighteen homicides, and six missing persons. Most criminologists believed the four gunmen were responsible for a great many more murders than were positively associated with them, and some estimates were in the hundreds.

"After the shooting, I was decorated for heroism, I was promoted to sergeant, I was on every news channel across America, and every politician who could get near to me – up to and including the President of the United States – wanted to win some votes by being filmed shaking hands with me," Logan added. "But since I shot two corrupt policemen, who killed my partner and who were trying to kill me, I've been treated like a pariah. My bosses, all the way up the chain of command, are trying to minimise media attention, as they don't want the general public to know we have corrupt policemen, and many of my brother police officers have started calling me *The Cop Killer*."

Blackmoor had established a therapeutic relationship with Logan and Logan was seizing the opportunity to vent his caged emotions.

"The first man I ever killed was a pimp and a drug pusher called Gregorio Taurez," Logan said. "It was before prostitution was legalised and regulated and before recreational drugs were state-controlled, and I was little more than a rookie."

Blackmoor had read Logan's file but didn't recall reading about the death of a man called Gregorio Taurez.

"Taurez was an evil man even by the standards of pimps and pushers of the time. He'd forced girls into prostitution by either intimidation or getting them addicted to heroin, and then he'd taken all their earnings," Logan continued. "Narcotics, Vice, and the Serious & Organised Crime Division had all tried to build cases against Taurez but he was always too slick for them. He knew who to threaten and who to kill, he knew which cops he could bribe, and he was working his way up through the ranks of a Colombian drug cartel and had some powerful allies."

Blackmoor had often noticed that when some of his patients recalled earlier stages of their lives, their speech patterns, facial expressions, and mannerisms reverted to the period of time they were evoking. They'd express themselves like frightened children or coy teenagers and now Logan was recollecting an episode from his early manhood, his demeanour had changed from a self-confident authority figure to a naive young man.

"Then Vice arrested twenty-three of his hookers in one night and seven of them agreed to testify that Taurez had forced them into prostitution," Logan said. "The seven girls were all given police protection at secret locations and my partner and I were assigned the job of protecting a girl called Matilda Mayfield. She was an actress from North Dakota who came to Hollywood to work in films but Taurez had abducted her, got her addicted to heroin, and forced her to work as a hooker. He'd also given her no end of beatings, but he gave all his girls regular beatings to make sure they worked hard, gave the money to him, and never tried to run."

Logan then paused to light a short cigar. Blackmoor didn't smoke but kept an ashtray in his office for the benefit his patients. Blackmoor's father had been a smoker and had usually smoked a pipe but, on special occasions, had smoked cigars. When Blackmoor was seven years old, he'd secretly smoked one of his father's cigars and had been horrendously sick and had never smoked again.

After Logan had lit his cigar, he continued: "Then Taurez found out where we were hiding his hookers, almost certainly from a cop he'd bribed or blackmailed, and all seven of the girls received recent photographs of their families with threats that if they testified their families would be made to suffer. The girls all refused to testify and Matilda got into a hot bath and slashed her wrists. My partner was a seasoned police officer who was showing me the ropes but he was more distraught by the incident than I was. We weren't on duty when Matilda received the photograph of her family and had slashed her wrists, and the police officers who were guarding her at the time had rushed her to hospital before she'd bleed to death, but we were still furious that Taurez had outsmarted us again."

Logan again paused to take a long pull on his cigar.

"At the same time that Vice was trying to build a case against Taurez, the FBI was investigating a man called Carlos Bandeira, who was the top dog of the drug cartel that Taurez was climbing the ranks of," Logan continued after he'd exhaled the smoke. "The FBI had an informant in Bandeira's organisation and Bandeira had offered to pay a small fortune to anyone who'd name the informer. While my partner and I were venting to each other that Taurez had outfoxed us again, a detective called Burt Drummond, who I suspected was on Bandeira's payroll, was eavesdropping on our conversation. Then I had an idea: while Drummond was secretly listening to us talking, I confided to my partner that Taurez was the FBI informant and we could never build a case against him because the FBI kept intervening on his behalf. I was hoping that Drummond would sell the information to Bandeira and Bandeira would take care of Taurez for us. I wasn't sure it would work but Taurez was dead within 24 hours."

Blackmoor had already said he understood that policemen frequently have to make choices between the lesser and the greater evil that would make the director of the CIA lose sleep, and the way Logan had dealt with Gregorio Taurez was one such case in point.

"It was what cops call *a public service homicide*," Logan said. "Taurez was dead and the world was a better place. The pimps and the pushers who filled the void left by Taurez weren't as slick or as vicious as he was, the pressure was taken off the FBI informant in

Bandeira's cartel, and Matilda Mayfield was weaned off heroin and went back to her life in North Dakota.

But Taurez was dead and I was responsible for his death; does that make me a murderer?"

"The only justifiable reason to take a human life is self-defence," Blackmoor replied. "And the only noble reason is to save an innocent life."

They were like-minded on the issue and Logan continued: "A couple of years after I was promoted to sergeant, I transferred to the Serious & Organised Crime Division. Police normally investigate a crime and then find the criminal, but in the Serious & Organised Crime Division, we investigated the criminal and then found the crime: the way the Feds investigated Al Capone and convicted him of tax evasion."

Blackmoor was aware that Logan had joined the Serious & Organised Crime Division shortly before narcotics were legalised and, at that time, career criminals had made gargantuan profits from dealing in drugs and were rich enough and powerful enough to bribe, intimidate, or assassinate politicians, jurists, and law enforcement officers, and the Serious & Organised Crime Division had an almost impossible job.

"About a year after I joined the division, narcotics were made state-controlled and the drug cartels were starting to feel the pinch and were moving into other illegal enterprises like human trafficking, extortion, and gunrunning; and a pack of hungry wolves are a lot more dangerous than a pack of well-fed wolves," Logan said. "We were trying to build a case against the Russian mafia when the Serious & Organised Crime Division was decimated by a bomb planted at our headquarters."

Blackmoor remembered the bombing vividly as it was all over the news and the reporters were stating the crime lords had cut the heart out of the Serious & Organised Crime Division and there was no one they feared or who could stand up to them.

"We were certain that an enforcer for the Russian mafia called Ivan Gorski, or *Ivan the Terrible* as he was dubbed, was responsible for the bombing, but we couldn't prove it," Logan continued. "He was the right-hand man and younger brother of Vladimir Gorski, the head of the Russian mafia in Los Angeles. I conspired with three men who were also in the Serious & Organised Crime Division but, like myself, were lucky enough not to be in the building when the bomb went off. We got hold of some military equipment that was favoured by the Colombian cocaine barons and we ambushed Ivan Gorski and three of his best men. I investigated the hit myself and submitted a report stating the Colombians were trying to muscle in on the Russians' territory. Vladimir Gorski believed it and he went to war with the Colombians. They almost destroyed each other, and we mopped up what was left."

Blackmoor had discussed this period of history with several people who work in law enforcement and the most commonly held opinion was that as the crooks were killing each other, the police didn't have to investigate, prosecute, and imprison them, which saved the taxpayers millions of dollars.

"I was promoted from sergeant to captain and ordered to rebuild the division, and over the years my team successfully investigated and prosecuted quite a few career criminals," Logan continued. "Then Jonathan Huxley, the District Attorney, asked me to take charge of the Internal Affairs Bureau and improve the performance of the whole LA police force. At first, I thought he was joking as I'd lost count of the number of times the IAB had investigated me, but he kept asking and eventually I agreed to the transfer. The first case I supervised for the IAB was also the last case I supervised for the Serious & Organised Crime Division: a sergeant in the LAPD called Matt Buchanan had infiltrated a gang of illegal arms dealers by taking bribes to warn them of any police activities that could impinge on their operation."

Blackmoor vaguely remembered hearing about the case.

"As a result of information ascertained by Buchanan, many of the gunrunners were successfully prosecuted and we seized millions of dollars of illegal arms," Logan said. "What most people don't know is Buchanan had already been taking bribes from the gunrunners for years before we caught him and I gave him a choice: he could serve a long prison sentence and spend the rest of his life in disgrace, or he could spy on, and testify against, the gunrunners and I'd claim it was prearranged with the Serious & Organised Crime Division that he'd take bribes from the illegal arms dealers to gain their trust."

"You conceived and implemented a course of action that was both productive and compassionate," Blackmoor responded.

"One of my innovations has been to offer police officers who are about to retire, but who've had long and exemplary careers, the chance to join the IAB and mentor younger police officers," Logan continued. "The Internal Affairs Bureau police the police and I've tried to make IAB officers the best of the best. And since I transferred to the IAB, the overall quality of the LA police force has improved, as reflected by increased arrest and conviction rates, fewer complaints of police brutality, and a drop in crime rates. But cops in all the other divisions still call the Internal Affairs Bureau 'The Rat Squad.'"

Chapter Eleven

Blackmoor thought he'd better check his emails and he pressed the button to engage the voice recognition facility on his laptop computer.

"Do I have any emails?" Blackmoor asked.

"You have ninety-two emails," his laptop computer replied. His laptop computer had the voice of a young lady with an American accent. "You have thirty-two emails from people who wish to engage your services as a psychiatrist and I forwarded their requests to your personal assistant. You have fifty-eight emails from alternative therapists requesting your endorsement and I have sent them all the polite refusal we composed."

Blackmoor received no end of emails from alternative therapists requesting his endorsement as a consequence of a lecture he'd given on alternative medicine and the work of Dr. Harriet Cameron.

Dr. Harriet Cameron, an oncologist (a physician who specializes in the diagnosis and treatment of cancer), became frustrated as many of her patients were approaching alternative therapists like psychic surgeons, faith healers, and homoeopaths, who she referred to as quacks, witch doctors, and snake oil salesmen. She had stated that all alternative therapies could be defined as forms of treatment that had failed clinical testing and had been discarded by orthodox medical science. She had added that alternative therapists not only encourage ill people to discontinue orthodox medical treatment, but some alternative therapists cause their clients harm with the treatments they offer, the most notorious example of which was an herbalist who poisoned thirty-seven of his clients.

To address the issue, Dr. Cameron employed a hypnotherapist to treat her patients for no other reason than to stop them from seeing other alternative therapists.

Much to Dr. Cameron's surprise, her patients became more optimistic, her terminally ill patients lived longer and were more productive with whatever time they had left, and the patients she cured improved more quickly.

Dr. Cameron attributed the improvement in the condition of her patients to the placebo effect: the placebo effect is a phenomenon wherein drugs and treatments that have no therapeutic value, and are often fake, make people feel better.

Dr. Cameron worked with several alternative therapists and found she obtained the best results if the therapist was caring, confident, and charismatic, no matter what nonsense they were conducting. The most caring, confident, and charismatic person she knew was her receptionist, and Dr. Cameron decided to teach her receptionist how to be a hypnotherapist; it wasn't difficult as the hypnotic inductions could be taught in a couple of hours and her receptionist only needed to know two suggestions: that the tumours were shrinking and the chemotherapy was not causing unpleasant side effects.

Dr. Cameron had written a book called *Hypnoses, Meditation and the Placebo Effect*, in which she had stated that although alternative therapies are only selling optimism, as long as they do not detract from orthodox medical care and the alternative therapist does not charge exorbitant fees, that's all well and good, and if one out of a hundred people receiving alternative therapies have miraculous recoveries that could possibly be attributed to the placebo effect, so much the better.

She had also proposed that alternative therapists should only be allowed to practise under the supervision of a medical doctor and as a result of Dr. Cameron's efforts, new legislation was introduced in many of the states of America and alternative therapists were only allowed to practise with the endorsement of an MD. The vast majority of medical doctors flatly refused to endorse any alternative therapists but fervently approved of the legislation as it put 95% of alternative therapists out of business.

During a lecture Blackmoor had given, he had said that, in his opinion, 99% of the placebo effect was self-deception as a result of the power of suggestion, but he had added in some circumstances the mind could have an effect on the body in a way that medical science had not yet identified or quantified. His lecture was recorded and put on the internet and as a consequence, hundreds of alternative therapists had contacted him to request his endorsement.

"Your accountant has asked if you would phone him," the laptop computer said.

"Remind me again tomorrow and I'll give him a ring."

"A pharmaceutical company has sent you a report about a new antipsychotic drug they are about to put on the market."

"Remind me about it tomorrow and I'll read the report, or you can read it to me."

Once Blackmoor had checked his emails and had switched off his laptop computer, he went to his kitchen to cook a meal as he had a dinner date with an ex-girlfriend. He anticipated it would be a romantic evening and it would have been more traditional to wine and dine his date at an expensive restaurant but Blackmoor very rarely ate at restaurants and generally prepared his own meals. Blackmoor had developed a fascination for martial arts and physical fitness when he was a boy and consequently had learnt about diet, nutrition, healthy eating, and cooking as part of his obsession.

Blackmoor's dinner date was with an African American girl called Scarlett Washington, whom he had not seen for over ten years. They had started dating when he was twenty-one and she was nineteen and she was already an international supermodel by then. The media had dubbed Scarlett "The Most Beautiful Girl in the World" when she was seventeen, and she had retained the epithet into her late twenties before a younger supermodel had ousted her.

Blackmoor had first met Scarlett at a very exclusive gymnasium, where they both had membership, and he had asked her if she wanted to go out on a date. Scarlett had told her parents and two older sisters that Blackmoor had asked her out, and when her family had learnt that Blackmoor was a medical student, they were delighted. Although as a supermodel, Scarlett earned ten times more than most consultant neurosurgeons, her family thought modelling was a very short-lived career and her father believed the game plan for any girl was to marry a good man who had a well-paid job and was from a respectable family. And Blackmoor ticked all the boxes. A great many young men had already asked Scarlett to go out with them, including photographers, male models, advertising executives, and an assortment of celebrities and businessmen, but her parents and older sisters had a lot of influence on her and they had never thought any of the young men were suitable.

Scarlett and Blackmoor's first date was at her place, so her parents could get to know Blackmoor and see if they approved of him, and their second date was at Blackmoor's family home. His parents were at a medical convention and Scarlett and Blackmoor had the house to themselves, and after they had eaten a meal that he had cooked, they watched a film on his widescreen TV.

After the film, he had casually asked if he could kiss her and she had said she didn't know how to kiss as this was her first date. Blackmoor realised she was a virgin and was shocked.

Blackmoor had lost his virginity when he was fifteen to a sixteen-year-old girl who was experienced, and he had had numerous lovers since. He'd studied and practised the art of lovemaking as intently as he'd studied the martial arts, as he wanted to excel as a lover, but he'd never deflowered a virgin because he believed it would be dishonourable to do so before committing to a long-term relationship.

Scarlett also had very mixed feelings about sex: she was understandably curious as her two older sisters and most of her friends were sexually active, and they had all said how wonderful sex was, but she was also apprehensive about her first time.

Blackmoor and Scarlett had both agreed it would be acceptable, appropriate, and pleasing to hug and kiss as long as the foreplay didn't end in coitus, and on their third date he had licked her ear and gently nibbled her earlobe, and, even though that was all he had done, she had an orgasm. At the time, Scarlett had said sex was better than she had hoped or imagined it would be, and she had added that her expectations had been quite high.

On their subsequent dates, Blackmoor had introduced additional methods of foreplay and had explored her beautiful, firm, curvaceous body by stroking, kissing, and licking every inch of her soft, smooth skin, while she was intoxicated with sexual ecstasy. He had taught her how to masturbate him and had suggested simultaneous mutual masturbation but she had said while he was stroking the lips of her vagina, she was delirious with ecstasy and was unable to control her actions, and for a few months they took turns masturbating each other as a conclusion to their foreplay.

About six months into their relationship, they had both said they loved each other and had agreed it was appropriate for Blackmoor to be her first lover. A sex therapist had told Blackmoor that the first time should be slow and gentle and should be preceded by a lot of foreplay. He had meticulously followed the advice he'd been given and as he penetrated Scarlett to engage in sexual intercourse, she hugged him, gave him a love bite on his shoulder, dug her heels into the backs of his knees, and pumped her hips until she'd climaxed.

She had said sexual intercourse was the nicest thing she had ever experienced and Blackmoor was delighted that Scarlett had enjoyed her first time, as quite a few women had told him their first time was both painful and unpleasant.

They became more sexually adventurous, although Scarlett never liked bondage or spanking and Blackmoor had never told her he was into the BDSM scene.

Their relationship had continued for another six months but Scarlett was trying to expand her career into acting and she had been offered a starring role in a film that was being shot in Europe. Blackmoor and Scarlett had kept in contact by webcam but their communications had gradually dwindled and after a few months she had offhandedly told Blackmoor she was dating a Spanish actor and, equally as casually, Blackmoor had told her he was seeing other girls. That was the end of their engagement and the last time they had spoken.

Since then, Scarlett had had numerous affairs and was married and divorced twice, once to a movie star and once to a producer, and her affairs, marriages, and divorces had been thoroughly scrutinized and reported on by the media. She had had many acting jobs but her acting was neither magnificent nor ridiculous and as her modelling career had declined, her acting career had also diminished.

Then about a week ago, Blackmoor had received an email from Scarlett stating she was back in Los Angeles and would like to meet with him. Blackmoor had suggested a date, a time, and a place, and Scarlett had agreed.

After Blackmoor had qualified as a medical doctor, he briefly lived in an apartment, but after his father had died, he had returned to the house he had grown up in to keep his mother company; he was an only child and he and his mother were very close. Two years later, his mother had died and Blackmoor continued to live at his family home and he was entertaining Scarlett at the same place they'd had their first unchaperoned date.

Blackmoor planned to seduce Scarlett before dinner, and, after a long relaxing evening, bed her again before she went home.

Blackmoor was both excited and apprehensive about meeting Scarlett again and decided to share his feelings with his *Dear Diary PC*. The *Dear Diary PC* was marketed as a best friend, a counsellor, and a confessor and although Blackmoor didn't believe computer technology had as yet evolved to a level where a computer could conduct psychotherapy, his Dear Diary PC was a good listener and he was certain it would keep his secrets. The *Dear Diary PC* could be linked to a laptop computer, and many people used it as a constant companion, but Blackmoor kept his *Dear Diary PC* completely insulated from the internet as he was afraid it might be hacked and he didn't want to risk a hacker learning the personal things he shared with his *Dear Diary PC*.

Blackmoor had named his *Dear Diary PC* "Pippa" after an English nanny he'd had as a child and he had programmed his *Dear Diary PC* to have an English accent that sounded as much like his nanny as possible. He did this primarily because he found the accent comforting but he also wanted his *Dear Diary PC* to have a very different voice to his other gadgets that could talk (all of which he'd given the accent of a young American girl) to ensure he wouldn't mistakenly share his intimate secrets with his laptop computer.

"Good afternoon, Pippa," Blackmoor said after he'd switched her on and typed in the access code.

"Good afternoon, Dominic," Pippa replied.

"I have a date with Scarlett this evening," Blackmoor said. "And I have mixed feelings about seeing her again."

"The last time we spoke, you told me you were excited about seeing Scarlett again but you were also afraid she'd be disappointed with you," Pippa replied.

"When I dated Scarlett, she was young, virginal, and naïve, but she's now quite worldly," Blackmoor said. "She's been married and divorced twice and has had affairs with some of the most legendary womanisers in the world, and she's not going to be as easily pleased as when we dated."

"Are you afraid your lovemaking will not be as marvellous as she remembers it to be, or do you feel in competition with the many womanisers Scarlett has had affairs with?" Pippa asked.

"Both!" Blackmoor replied.

"Your date with Scarlett might be a challenge, but every challenge is an adventure, so do your best and enjoy the challenge and the adventure," Pippa replied.

Blackmoor thanked Pippa for her shrewd advice and returned to cooking the meal for his dinner date with Scarlett.

The Spectre

Scarlett had been wined and dined at some of the most expensive restaurants in the world and had eaten meals prepared by many internationally acclaimed chefs and, although food wasn't just fuel to Blackmoor and he liked to cook and eat good-tasting meals, his culinary skills couldn't possibly compete with the world-famous chefs who had cooked for Scarlett. As well as that, Scarlett was also a connoisseur of fine wines and Blackmoor never consumed alcohol. But, although the thought of being bested by one or more of Scarlett's ex-lovers horrified Blackmoor, the thought of being outdone by one or more of her chefs caused him no unease.

Scarlett was punctual and after he'd invited her into his home and told her she was still as beautiful as she ever was, he suggested giving her a guided tour of his house to show her the changes he'd made. They both commented on the features of his home he had changed since Scarlett was last there and they also commented on the features of his home he had left exactly as they were.

As it was where Scarlett had had her first sexual experiences, had lost her virginity, and had had countless orgasms, the house had almost as many fond memories for Scarlett as it did for Blackmoor.

The house and garden were picture-perfect, and as Scarlett knew Blackmoor loathed housework, gardening, and do-it-yourself, she correctly surmised that he employed a housekeeper, a gardener, and a decorator.

He showed her his study, which had also been his father's study, and she was touched to see that Blackmoor had kept some gifts she had given him while they were dating: a mouse mat, a letter opener, and a paperweight. Printed at the bottom of the mouse mat were the words "THE THREE WISER MONKEYS." Above the words was a picture of three monkeys and they all had their hands over their mouths but had their ears and eyes open. Printed at the top of the mouse mat was a motto stemming from Yorkshire, England: *Hear all, see all, say nowt.* The meaning of the motto was to hear everything, see everything, but say nothing. The design of the mouse mat was inspired by the Japanese pictorial maxim the three wise monkeys, who *hear no evil, see no evil, speak no evil,* but in the opinion of the manufacturer of the mouse mat, the three wiser monkeys *Hear all, see all, say nowt.*

While she had been on a modelling gig in Cornwall, England, she had bought Blackmoor a combined letter opener and paperweight. The letter opener was designed to look like King Arthur's magic sword, *Excalibur,* and was sheathed standing upright in a flat-bottomed stone that was big enough and heavy enough to be used as a paperweight. The paperweight and letter opener were designed thusly because, according to legend, King Arthur drew his magic sword from a stone. As almost all written communication was done via email, Blackmoor would have little or no use for either a letter opener or a paperweight, but he kept them for sentimental reasons.

Quite premeditatedly, Blackmoor made the concluding part of the tour his bedroom, where he hoped to seduce Scarlett. As soon as they'd entered his bedroom, Scarlett put her arms around Blackmoor and kissed him on the mouth. They fell onto Blackmoor's bed and their lovemaking was passionate but not rough: exactly the way Scarlett liked it.

After they'd made love, Blackmoor served dinner and they swapped stories about what they'd been doing for the last ten years.

"My accountant tells me I'll soon have to declare bankruptcy," Scarlett said.

For a moment, Blackmoor thought she was joking and when he realised she was being serious, he was surprised by how casually she had made the statement.

"You were the highest paid model in the world for over a decade," Blackmoor said. "And you married and divorced two millionaires. Where did all the money go?"

"While I was earning the big bucks, I developed some very expensive tastes," she replied. "But a couple of years ago, I went out of fashion and the modelling and acting jobs petered out. And to maintain the lifestyle I'd grown accustomed to, I ran up some large debts."

In Blackmoor's opinion, Scarlett was still as beautiful as she ever was, but he understood that models could go out of vogue as quickly as the products they're promoting, and now Scarlett was no longer fashionable, she wouldn't be able to earn the enormous sums of money she once had.

"Now my agent tells me the only gigs he can get for me are nude modelling for art classes," Scarlett said.

"What are you going to do?" Blackmoor asked.

"I bought my parents a big house in a very respectable neighbourhood when I was rich, and they've said I can live with them for as long as I like," she replied. "So, I'll never be homeless or hungry."

Scarlett looked troubled and, after a thoughtful pause, continued: "My agent has made a suggestion."

She again looked distressed and her troubled pensive pauses were alarming Blackmoor.

"What does he want you to do?" Blackmoor asked.

"He wants to hire a ghostwriter to write my life story," Scarlett said. "My agent said the money I make from my autobiography would clear my debts and could possibly re-start my acting career."

"Why do you find that distressing?" Blackmoor asked.

"I've married and divorced two millionaires, and I've had affairs with quite a few A-list celebrities, and my agent wants me to write a *kiss and tell* story," Scarlett replied. "Almost all of the men I've had sex with have regarded me as a *trophy fuck* and have bragged about bedding me to anyone who'd listen, so I have no remorse about telling everything about them, but you were my first lover and you've never talked about it, and I feel guilty about telling everyone about you."

"It would be an honour and a privilege to be mentioned in your memoirs," he said. Blackmoor never crowed about his sexual conquests but he was flattered and delighted when the women he'd seduced bragged about having sex with him.

Scarlett mused to herself that if Blackmoor was pleased she was going to mention him in her autobiography, he'd be ecstatic when he read it: she was going to say he was the best lover she'd ever had to belittle and annoy her ex-husbands and many of her ex-lovers.

They continued to reminisce and Scarlett recalled that Blackmoor had frequently given her massages and had taught her how to give a massage. He asked her if she'd like him to give her a massage that evening and she was only too pleased to accept his offer.

As Scarlett lay face down on the bed, Blackmoor admired her buttocks and pondered how thrilling it would be to tie her to the bed and give her a spanking. He limited himself to giving her a gentle pat on her bottom, which, from past experience, he knew she found flattering.

Blackmoor's desire to give Scarlett a spanking but limiting himself to giving her a gentle pat on the backside, reminded him of a discussion he'd had with his father when he was fourteen years old. His father had told him all about the mechanics of procreation, contraception, and safe sex, most of which he already knew, and his father had also taught him about BDSM role-playing games and safe words, which he was completely ignorant about but the thought was important to know. Blackmoor also vividly recalled that his father had added there was no reason or excuse for a man to strike a lady, with the exception of S&M role-playing games with a pre-agreed safe word. At the time, Blackmoor thought that all fathers had this conversation with their sons but a few years later he wondered if his father had been monitoring his computer activity and had discovered he'd been watching bondage and corporal punishment films on the internet, which he had used as masturbatory aids.

The Spectre

A couple of years later, when Blackmoor was sixteen, a girl in his school who was remarkably attractive, who was thoroughly spoilt by her well-to-do parents, and who even the school counsellor had described as *bitchy and entitled*, had bragged she could get a date with any boy she wanted. She was also sixteen and usually dated boys who were three to five years older than her but she had told all her school friends she was going to a pending party with Blackmoor. One lunch time, she sat opposite Blackmoor in the school cafeteria and chatted with him very generally about the party and then cunningly accepted his invitation to go with him, when he hadn't actually asked her. She expected Blackmoor to jump at the chance to go out with her but he apologised for the misunderstanding and said he already had a date for the party. In a rage, she violently slapped Blackmoor across the face, much to the amusement of his friends and hers. She tried to slap him again but he blocked her hand and she responded by throwing a glass of milk in his face, closely followed by her whole lunch tray.

Blackmoor walked out of the cafeteria and went to the restroom to clean up without retaliating. When Blackmoor's father learnt of the incident from the school counsellor, he spoke to his son and said he was very proud that he hadn't hit the girl back. Blackmoor's parents were always lavish with their praise of him regarding all his endeavours but this was the one and only time Blackmoor recalled his father had tears of pride in his eyes.

Chapter Twelve

It was Wednesday afternoon and Blackmoor was working at his office. His last appointment of the day was with Ms. Catherine Falconer, who was a legendary defence attorney. She had never lost a case and was renowned for getting very rich clients and not-guilty verdicts. Her most famous client was a rock star called Spike Zaroff, who had shot four people at a party while he was high on a combination of narcotics and alcohol. In court, one of Zaroff's groupies had claimed she had furtively laced his drink with a hallucinogenic drug and, while hallucinating, he had snatched a pistol from one of his bodyguards and started shooting. None of the four people he had shot had been killed and Zaroff had already agreed to pay for their medical care and to compensate them for their injuries, but even if he'd murdered all four of them, he would have received a not-guilty verdict.

Falconer had represented Zaroff in court on a few subsequent occasions but after a few years he went out of fashion as a rock star and as he was no longer earning the vast sums of money he once had, he could no longer afford to employ her. Shortly after declaring bankruptcy, Zaroff had savagely beaten his current live-in girlfriend and had given her a fractured skull and an assortment of other injuries. He was allocated a court-appointed lawyer to defend him but he was found guilty of *assault with intent to kill* and received a ten-year prison sentence.

Blackmoor had worked with Falconer on a prior occasion when she had retained his services as an expert witness: a young man called Timothy Fitzharris Berkeley Jr., who was from a very well-to-do family, had bludgeoned seven women with a wooden cudgel. On dark nights, he'd lurk in places of concealment, and when unaccompanied women walked by, he'd jump out of the shadows and attack them. None of the women he'd clubbed had died but many had been seriously injured. When Berkeley was caught, he claimed he was hearing voices that commanded him to attack women. He was examined by several psychiatrists, and many thought he was genuinely psychotic, but others had pointed out that Berkeley had been functioning quite well with his studies at an Ivy League university, he only attacked women at places that had no CCTV cameras, and he would never attack women who were escorted by men, and they expressed the opinion that Berkeley was a psychopath and was pretending to be psychotic to enable his moneyed family to send him to a psychiatric facility, where he could engineer an early release and avoid a long prison sentence.

Berkeley's family had retained Falconer to defend him in court and she understood that as he was from a privileged background and was the heir to a large fortune, he'd provoke a lot of envy and resentment from the jurors. She also realised that as his attacks were against women of all ages and ethnic groups, the jurors would perceive his victims as mothers, daughters, sisters, wives, girlfriends, and even grandmothers and would be delighted to give Berkeley a guilty verdict.

In response to a very difficult situation, Falconer had employed Blackmoor as an expert witness as he was good looking, had a charming manner, and, as he had already had a few TV appearances by then, the jury would be aware of his prestige as a forensic psychiatrist and would have a lot of respect for his opinion. Whenever possible, Falconer would utilise the *Halo Effect: the tendency people have to believe that positive traits cluster together, and if someone is attractive, they will also be honourable and intelligent.* Falconer would select her expert witnesses largely by how pleasing they were to the eye, and as Blackmoor was both good looking and charismatic, she knew he could win the case for her.

Blackmoor examined Berkeley and concluded he was a paranoid schizophrenic and recommended he be detained in a hospital for the criminally insane and be treated with antipsychotic medication.

In court, when Blackmoor gave evidence as an expert witness, Falconer finished her extensive examination with one simple question: "Is Timothy Fitzharris Berkeley Jr. mad, or is he bad?"

"He's mad," Blackmoor replied.

Falconer knew she'd won the case with that one simple question and answer.

Berkeley was found not guilty by reason of insanity and was sentenced to be detained at a maximum-security unit for the criminally insane until a team of court appointed psychiatrists deemed he was fit to return to society.

During their collaboration, Blackmoor had had three meetings with Falconer, and on all three occasions, Blackmoor had had to go to her office, but now Falconer had come to see him. She had phoned Blackmoor's assistant that morning and had asked to make an urgent appointment and had stressed she wanted to see Blackmoor as a patient and not for professional collaboration. Blackmoor usually saw a patient every hour on the hour from 9 am to 4 pm, with a one-hour lunch break at noon, and finished work at 5 pm, but if he had to see a patient urgently and his appointment planner was jam-packed, he'd see the patient at 5 pm, and Blackmoor had arranged to see Falconer at 5 pm the same day she had requested an appointment.

Blackmoor's personal assistant ushered Falconer into his office and he was very surprised by how little attention Falconer had paid to her appearance. Whenever he'd seen her in the past, she had taken more time and trouble with her clothes, her hair, and her makeup than a fashion model, but now she was wearing a tracksuit, no makeup, and she'd let her hair down. She was also wearing dark glasses and Blackmoor suspected she was trying to disguise herself as she didn't want anyone to know she was seeing a psychiatrist.

"How can I help you?" Blackmoor asked.

"As you're fully aware, I'm an exceptional defence attorney," Falconer replied. She removed her dark glasses as she spoke and her eyes were red and swollen from crying. "I've never lost a case and I've seldom crossed swords with a prosecutor who I considered to be a worthy opponent. And I'm honour bound to do my very best for my clients, even if I think they're the scum of the earth and as guilty as sin."

Blackmoor fully understood the point she was making as a result of conversations he'd had with District Attorney Jonathan Huxley: as a prosecutor, Huxley could offer people he was prosecuting lenient sentences if he believed they were deserving of compassion. And when he was a young deputy district attorney, if he was forced to prosecute a drug addict, or anyone he believed to be a victim of an unfair legal system, he didn't try as hard as he could have to win the case, but, as a defence attorney, Falconer had to do her very best for her clients no matter how morally reprehensible or obnoxious they were.

"I was hired by a man called Harvey Kelleher, who's the president of a major corporation," she said. "He was accused of drugging and raping a girl called Molly Macqueen, which was the latest allegation in a series of accusations of sexual harassment by her and several of Kelleher's other subordinate female colleagues. The case went to trial, and by the time I'd finished cross-examining her, the jury thought she'd been stalking Kelleher and her accusation of rape was the latest manifestation of her obsession with him."

Blackmoor had heard quite a few horror stories about Falconer's formidable, devious, and merciless cross-examination techniques.

Falconer started to weep and dried her eyes with a tissue before she continued: "After I'd finished questioning her, she went home and hanged herself."

Chapter Thirteen

Blackmoor and Vikki had arranged to see each other for a role-playing game that evening and when he arrived at her apartment, she had asked him to help himself to a cup of coffee while she got changed. He'd just sat down and started to sip the coffee when Vikki emerged from her bedroom dressed like a schoolgirl. She was wearing a white blouse, a necktie, a pleated mini skirt, black seamed stockings and a suspender belt, and she had tied her hair in bunches with thick ribbons. The ribbons were tied in big bows and had the same tartan pattern as her pleated mini skirt and necktie. She had tied her hair in bunches on many previous occasions but this was the first time she'd used thick ribbons tied in big bows; Blackmoor thought it was very erotic and made a mental note to tell her to keep doing it.

"Over my knee!" Blackmoor commanded. When she was playing *The Stuck-up Bitch*, he'd put her across his knee, but when she was playing *The Spoilt Brat*, he'd bark orders at her and she'd put herself across his knee.

She curtseyed clumsily at the door and then walked over to Blackmoor. He was sitting on a straight-backed chair that had no arms and she bent over his lap.

"You need to be disciplined: punished: spanked!" Blackmoor said sternly as he started to spank her across the seat of her mini skirt.

As he slapped her, he reprimanded her: "You're a wayward little minx!"

After about fifty smacks, he flipped up her mini-skirt and spanked her bottom over her tight white panties.

"Ouch!" she yelped, even though the slap wasn't very hard. "That really hurts Sir; not much more."

"You're a petulant little brat!" Blackmoor said as he slapped her bottom.

"Ouch!" she yelped. "Please stop Sir; I've learnt my lesson."

When Blackmoor judged it was the right time to progress the spanking to the next level, he hooked his index finger under the waistband of Vikki's panties and slowly and tantalizingly pulled them down.

"Please don't take my panties down," she pleaded.

Blackmoor lowered her panties to the tops of her thighs and recommenced the spanking.

After he'd given her about fifty love pats, he ordered her to pull up her panties and stand in the corner.

Vikki got up from across his knees, pulled up her panties, curtseyed, and walked to the corner of the room. While she was facing the wall, she rubbed the seat of her panties with both hands. Her bottom wasn't hurting but she knew Blackmoor enjoyed watching her rub her butt.

He admired the view for a couple of minutes and then ordered Vikki to return to the centre of the room and to bend over and grasp her ankles. She obeyed his commands and as she bent over, she kept her legs straight and flipped up her mini skirt to present her panties, suspender belt, and stocking tops.

Blackmoor again paused to admire the view as the bent-over position emphasised her long legs and made her look especially sexy.

Blackmoor had brought a large leather paddle and he used it to give Vikki a whack across her backside. The paddle had a large surface area and caused less of a sting than a slipper, a hairbrush, or a cane, but it made a loud dramatic smack when he whacked her with it. Vikki yelped and Blackmoor didn't know if it was a yelp of pleasure, pain, surprise, or all three. He gave her another five swats with the paddle with long pauses between whacks and she yelped with every swat but didn't move.

"Take off your shoes, your blouse, and your skirt!" Blackmoor commanded.

She took off her flat sensible shoes, which she placed near the wall, and then took off her necktie, blouse, and mini skirt, all of which she neatly folded and placed on the couch.

"Bend over the seat of the chair!" he ordered.

Vikki lay face down across the padded seat of the straight-backed chair with her hands and feet touching the floor. He slowly lowered her panties to the tops of her thighs so her magnificent butt was framed by her suspender belt, panties, and stocking tops.

Blackmoor again paused to gaze at Vikki and if she had been playing *The Irresistible Temptress*, he would have said: *If God had made anything sexier than your butt, he kept it for himself.*

"Green Light," Vikki said quickly: she wanted the game to move on but she didn't want to kill the mood.

He responded by paddling her bottom briskly but with little force and she twitched and squealed with every whack.

Eventually, Blackmoor stopped beating her and barked some more orders at her: "Kneel on the chair!"

Vikki scrambled to her feet and knelt on the seat of the chair.

"Stick your butt out!" he commanded.

She obediently thrust out her hips and he started to paddle her bottom, and before each whack, he'd fondle, tickle, and pat her backside. This was the climax of the spanking and Blackmoor paddled Vikki until her butt had started to turn pink.

"Go into the bedroom, take off your bra and panties, and lay on the bed!" he ordered.

She walked into her bedroom, removed her underwear, climbed onto her bed, laid on her back, and covered her eyes with her hands in a childlike manner.

The Spectre

Blackmoor was wearing a tracksuit and hurriedly disrobed.

Once he was naked, he pounced on Vikki and started gently biting her breasts and nipples.

"Don't do that Sir!" she pleaded.

"Oh, shop Shir," Vikki began to slur her words as she became delirious with ecstasy, and then she just squealed.

Blackmoor then put on a condom and mounted her, and she climaxed quite noisily; Vikki was a screamer and she knew from her prior liaisons with Blackmoor that he liked to hear her scream with ecstasy and to please and flatter him, she exaggerated her screams rather than stifled them.

Chapter Fourteen

Blackmoor's 3 pm appointment was with a motivational psychologist called Dr. Annabelle Shelley, who managed one of the biggest advertising agencies in the world, which she had built from scratch, and who had authored a book about advertising called *Tell the Truth; Sell the Truth*. Blackmoor had read *Tell the Truth; Sell the Truth* as, although it was primarily a beginner's guide to advertising, it was also a textbook about motivational psychology and Blackmoor thought her book had several innovative concepts, unlike the majority of new textbooks that are entirely a rehash of the old ones.

She later wrote an autobiography called *Making Lemonade*, which Blackmoor had read to gain a deeper understanding of *Tell the Truth; Sell the Truth.* All psychologists use a degree of introspection in their understanding of other people's behaviour, including Sigmund Freud, the trailblazer of psychoanalysis, and all theories in psychology are influenced by the personalities of the theorists who formulated them.

The title of her autobiography, *Making Lemonade,* was inspired by the proverbial phrase *When life gives you lemons, make lemonade.*

Shelley was from a privileged background but her father had sexually abused her throughout her childhood and early teens. She was married at eighteen to a man called Raymond Brewster, who she later discovered was a psychopath and a brute. He had viciously beaten her on numerous occasions and as a result of her traumatic childhood and abusive marriage, she became addicted to alcohol, prescription drugs, and recreational drugs.

During one particularly savage beating, one of her neighbours had called the police, and when the police had intervened, Brewster had also attacked them. Brewster was convicted of assaulting his wife and of assaulting the police officers and was given a prison sentence. Shelley was hospitalised for the injuries she'd sustained at the hands of her husband and once discharged from the hospital, was transferred to a psychiatric unit to be cured of her addictions and to receive counselling to help her come to terms with her traumatic childhood and abusive marriage. As one of her addictions was cocaine that she'd purchased at a government ran centre, the state picked up the tab for her treatment.

Once Shelley was cured of her addictions, had divorced Brewster, and was free of her demons, she resumed her education and attained a Ph.D. in psychology. She had started working for an advertising agency and had proved to be exceptionally good at creating and implementing advertising campaigns and eventually started her own advertising agency. Her most successful advertising campaign had been for the *Quincannon Heavy Duty Industrial Strength Clothing Company*, who had offered her one hundred thousand dollars to advertise their goods. After reviewing their merchandise, she said she didn't want the fee in cash but would take one hundred thousand dollars of shares in their company as she believed she could radically improve their sales figures. The company directors were pleased and impressed by her optimism and enthusiastically agreed to her proposal. Shelley recommended they change the name of their company from *Quincannon Heavy Duty Industrial Strength Clothing* to *Quality Pays,* and in the advertising campaign she masterminded, she emphasised that although their products may cost three or four or five times more than other clothing manufacturers, as they last more than ten times longer, in the long run, they'd save the customers money, as quality pays. Shelley also recommended they print the *Quality Pays* logo on their goods so the people who buy and wear their clothing would be giving their company free advertising. The campaign was more successful than anyone had hoped or imagined it would be and their sales figures increased dramatically. *Quality Pays* expanded into a great many other heavy duty industrial strength goods, all of which displayed the *Quality Pays* logo, and the one hundred thousand dollars in company shares they had paid Shelley was currently worth about ten million dollars.

Blackmoor and Shelley had once worked on the same project but neither of them knew of the other's involvement at the time: Bram Goldstein, the President of the United States of America, was going into negotiations with President Daryl Chin, the head of state of the People's Republic of China, and one of President Goldstein's advisers had suggested he engage a psychologist to profile the Chinese head of state and predict how he would behave and recommend approaches that would generate the most productive outcomes during the negotiations. President Goldstein considered the suggestion and decided to employ two people: Dr. Dominic Blackmoor and Dr. Annabelle Shelley.

President Goldstein had chosen Blackmoor because the Director of the FBI had said Blackmoor was his best profiler, and he had chosen Shelley because she was the most acclaimed practitioner in advertising in the USA and it was her job to predict what people were going to do and foresee ways of manipulating their actions.

Blackmoor and Shelley submitted their profiles of President Chin and they both made more or less the same predictions and recommendations, which delighted President Goldstein as experts frequently contradict each other, making it difficult to know whose advice to take. And their predictions of how President Chin would act and react were astonishingly accurate.

"I read the article you authored about feminism and the emancipation of women," Shelley said as soon as Blackmoor's personal assistant had escorted her into his office.

The article she was referring to read:

Throughout human history, women have been regarded as property to be bought, sold, or taken by force, and once owned, they were chattels to be used and abused by the men who owned them. The suffragettes, feminists, and women's liberationists who fought for equal rights for women were freedom fighters the equal of black Americans who fought in the Union Army during the American Civil War to end black slavery in the United States of America.

When famines, wars, and plagues were almost completely eliminated, and people started living longer as a result of strides in medical science, human overpopulation became a greater danger to life on Earth than global warming or pollution because as more and more land had to be converted to agriculture to feed the ever-growing population of humans, more and more plant and animal species would be driven to extinction, and, eventually, the Earth would not be able to produce enough food to feed the number of humans living on it and there would be worldwide famine. The most effective way to control human overpopulation was found to be to educate and empower women, as most career women only have one child, more career women have no children than have two, and very few have three or more. All over the world, including the Muslim nations, girls were educated as rigorously as boys to enable them to develop careers and in 2106 the world's population of humans contracted for the first time in centuries and has contracted a little every year ever since.

As women are being better educated, they have become a larger percentage of politicians, executives, and managers, although women have never reached the 50% level in executive or management roles as they do not have the testosterone fuelled ambition that men have and, in my opinion, the world has become a better place as a direct result of women being in positions of power and authority, as women have a greater capacity for empathy and compassion than do men.

Apparently, the article he had written had greatly impressed Shelley and Blackmoor wondered if that was the reason she had chosen him to be her therapist.

"You stated in the article that women's liberationists were freedom fighters the equal of black Americans who fought to end black slavery in the United States," Shelley said as they walked to the armchairs in his office. "Were you suggesting that women were slaves or a persecuted minority group?"

"Both," Blackmoor replied as they were sitting down.

She appeared to approve of his answer and Blackmoor commenced their session.

"How can I help you?" he asked.

"Have you read my autobiography?" she answered his question with a question.

"Yes," Blackmoor replied.

"Then you know that as a child, I was sexually molested by my father, I was regularly beaten and raped by my first husband, and I was once addicted to alcohol, recreational drugs, and prescription medication," Shelley said. "After I was cured of my addictions, I studied psychology to understand why my father and first husband did the terrible things they did to me."

Everything she had said so far was in her autobiography, and Blackmoor had already told her he had read it, but if she wanted to vent, it was her session.

"As a motivational psychologist, I've learnt how to get into people's heads and how to push their buttons," she continued. "And one key factor I have to take into account while I'm planning an advertising campaign is that men and women think and feel very differently, and all men have a streak of callousness and misogyny ingrained in them."

"I think what you're saying is as women have a greater depth of feeling than do men, from the feminine point of view, a lot of masculine behaviour appears psychopathic, and from the masculine point of view, a lot of feminine behaviour appears quixotic," Blackmoor responded.

"No," she said. "What I'm saying is all men are bastards; except you."

Blackmoor wasn't surprised by her statement that he was the only man in the world who wasn't a bastard, as he'd heard similar remarks from several of his female patients: it was a well-

The Spectre

documented phenomenon that many people with mental health problems give their therapists a godlike status.

"I met my second husband while I was working for an advertising agency, and about eighteen months into our marriage, I got horrendously drunk at an office party," she continued. "My colleagues phoned my husband and asked him to come and collect me, but just after they phoned him, I lost consciousness, and they called for an ambulance. My husband arrived at the same time as the paramedics and went to the hospital with me. They kept me in overnight and did some blood tests, which revealed I'd also taken some recreational drugs with the alcohol, although I had no recollection of doing so. The following day, my husband took me home, and as soon as we got home, he put me across his knee and spanked me. It was the most humiliating experience of my life: I was in my thirties and a company executive and I was having my butt smacked like a naughty child. I told him if he ever beat me again, I'd leave him."

Blackmoor nodded in agreement. Blackmoor had spanked a great many women but only as a sex game with a pre-agreed safe word, and he had never and would never beat a woman purely to punish her.

"Just over a year later, I went for a girls' night out with four of my friends, and I woke up in hospital," Shelley continued. "As soon as my husband got me home, he put me over his knee and spanked me, and while he was spanking me, he told me if I ever drank again, even a single glass of wine, I'd get more of the same."

She paused to drink some water; Blackmoor always kept a jug of water and some glasses within easy reach in case one of his patients, or he himself, had a dry throat.

"The next day, after my husband went to work, I packed my bags and left him," she said. "When my husband learnt I was divorcing him, he pleaded with me not to leave him. Most of my friends thought I was overreacting and my best friend strongly advised me to take him back and give up drinking. When I asked her if she'd like it if her significant other had spanked her and forbade her to drink, she replied, 'I like a man to be a man.' There's a common masculine myth that all women like to be dominated, and I'm sure, like my best friend, many women do, but I'm not one of them."

Shelley again paused to drink from the glass she was holding.

"After we separated, I became very sexually promiscuous," she said. "Are you appalled?"

"No," Blackmoor replied.

Shelley paused to study Blackmoor's facial expressions to look for signs of approval or disapproval: although Blackmoor had said he wasn't appalled because she'd had casual sex with numerous partners, she wanted some confirmation of his sincerity. Once she was satisfied Blackmoor was genuinely not disapproving of her actions, she continued: "One of the last remaining vestiges of the inequality of the sexes is that men are lionised for being sexually promiscuous, and women are vilified for the same reason. And a great many people, including some of my female friends, were shocked and disgusted that I had casual sex with numerous partners."

Blackmoor agreed there were double standards regarding sexual promiscuity and men were hero-worshipped for being sexually promiscuous, whereas women were pilloried for exactly the same reason.

"I've had lesbian tendencies since puberty but I'd never acted on them, or even admitted that I had them, until I separated from my second husband," Shelley said. "After which, I had as many female lovers as male lovers. None of my affairs were exclusive or lasted for very long until I met a girl called Jasmine. Our relationship began as purely physical but we gradually saw more and more of each other until she moved into my house and we were living together. We've lived together for just over a year and I now think of her as being as much a part of me as my own beating heart."

Blackmoor had lost count of the number of people he'd heard refer to their significant other as their *other half*, but it was something he had never personally experienced.

"It's the first time in my life I've bonded with someone as deeply as that and it wasn't a feeling I'd had with either of my husbands," she continued. "I asked Jasmine to marry me and she said a part of her really wanted to say yes but she had always wanted to have a husband and children and she wanted some time apart to think things through."

Shelley again paused to drink from the glass she was holding and she gulped back three big swallows of water as if she imagined it was something stronger like gin.

"Jasmine completes me," Shelley said. "I don't know what I'll do if she doesn't come back to me."

Chapter Fifteen

Blackmoor received a text from Ramona Cortez requesting that he visit her at her apartment as soon as possible, but she did not explain why she wanted to see him. It was Sunday afternoon, and Blackmoor had nothing planned, and he immediately went to her apartment.

Ramona opened her front door wearing a bra, panties, black seamed stockings and a suspender belt; an ensemble she knew Blackmoor found sexy. Blackmoor was a tad surprised as she had given him no indication it was a bootie call. She also had tears on her cheeks, red puffy eyes from crying, and was holding a half empty glass of red wine. Ramona appeared tipsy but as she seldom consumed alcohol, it would only take a couple of glasses of wine to make her slightly drunk.

She invited Blackmoor into her apartment and asked him to view a video recording she was watching on TV. The video recording was of a girl walking along a beach and being filmed from various points of view while a man was singing *The Girl from Ipanema*:

Tall and tanned and young and lovely,

the girl from Ipanema goes walking

and when she passes, each one she passes goes ahhh.

When she walks, she's like a samba that swings so cool and sways so gently

that when she passes, each one she passes goes ahhh.

Ooh, but I watch her so sadly; how can I tell her I love her?

Yes I would give my heart gladly,

but each day, when she walks to the sea

she looks straight ahead, not at me.

*Tall and tanned and young and lovely,
the girl from Ipanema goes walking
and when she passes, I smile, but she doesn't see.
She just doesn't see, she never sees me.*

The very attractive girl being filmed was indeed tall and tanned and young and lovely.

"Who's she?" Blackmoor asked at the conclusion of the song.

"That was me when I was eighteen," Ramona replied. "A friend of mine was a singer and he'd recorded *The Girl from Ipanema* and he'd asked me to appear in the promotional video. I told him to get a professional model but he said I was perfect to play the girl from Ipanema."

After viewing the promotional video, Blackmoor strongly agreed with him.

"It's my birthday today," Ramona said. "I've just turned fifty and I'm a fat old cow!"

Now Blackmoor understood why Ramona had summoned him and why she was wearing an ensemble she knew he found sexy: it was her fiftieth birthday and she was afraid of becoming old and she needed to be reassured she was still sexually attractive.

"You're a very beautiful woman," Blackmoor said.

"I'm a fat old cow!"

"You're voluptuous, curvaceous, buxom."

"Don't patronise me!"

As a hard-and-fast rule, Blackmoor never participated in BDSM role-playing games without a prearranged safe word, but if he was playing with a submissive partner he was very au fait with, and if the situation facilitated it, he would do something that bent the rules and spiced up the game.

Blackmoor had sat down to watch the video recording and he got to his feet before speaking: "Tell me you're the sexiest bitch imaginable or I'll spank you until you do!"

In place of a safe word, Ramona would have to say *I'm the sexiest bitch imaginable* to make Blackmoor stop spanking her.

Blackmoor's statement had an incredibly sobering effect on Ramona and she stood square to him before replying: "You wouldn't dare!"

Blackmoor immediately threw her over his shoulder and started carrying her towards her bedroom.

Ramona hadn't been carried over someone's shoulder since she was a child and it thrilled her to be overpowered.

While Blackmoor was carrying Ramona into her bedroom, he started slapping her bottom. Blackmoor had spanked Ramona while she was lying face down on her bed, while she was across his knee, while she was bent over a chair, and in a few other positions, but this was the first time he'd spanked her while she was over his shoulder. As she was enjoying the new experience, on reaching her bedroom, instead of lowering Ramona onto her bed, Blackmoor continued to spank her while she was over his shoulder.

To add variety to the liaison, Blackmoor took hold of her left ankle, removed her slipper, and tickled the sole of her foot. Ramona was very ticklish and liked to be tickled.

Then, without putting her down, Blackmoor walked around her bedroom, searching for something. He soon found what he was looking for: a thin leather belt. After carrying Ramona back to her bed, Blackmoor put her down, sat on the corner of her bed, and put her face down across his lap. He then pulled her hands behind her back and tied her wrists together with the leather belt; Blackmoor hadn't brought his bondage equipment with him and had to improvise. Ramona was still wearing her right slipper and he removed it from her foot and used it to give her a whack on her bottom before resting the slipper between her shoulder blades.

As was his custom, Blackmoor then gave Ramona a light warm-up spanking, and while he was spanking her, she kept still with her eyes closed and a smile on her face.

After about fifty love pats, Blackmoor seized her right ankle and started to tickle her foot, and while he tickled her, she laughed uncontrollably and struggled frantically against Blackmoor's grip and the belt that was binding her wrists.

Then, while Blackmoor continued to hold Ramona across his lap, he alternately spanked her bottom with his hand or her slipper, tickled her feet, or stroked her vagina through her panties.

At irregular intervals, Blackmoor would surprise Ramona by pinching her bottom, and she would respond with a yelp of delight.

"I'm the sexiest bitch imaginable," she said when she thought the BDSM foreplay had reached a peak.

He lifted Ramona from off his lap and laid her face down on her bed. Before untying her hands, he took off his own clothes and took a condom out of his wallet (he always carried condoms in his wallet). Blackmoor then pulled off her panties, unclasped her bra, untied her wrists, rolled her onto her back, and started kissing her on her mouth. While they were kissing, he pulled off her bra and gently fondled her breasts.

"Have me now," Ramona whispered.

Blackmoor put on a condom and mounted her. She was a screamer and climaxed quite noisily and Blackmoor was extremely flattered by the positive feedback.

After they had both climaxed, Blackmoor fell asleep. He was awoken by the sound of *The Girl from Ipanema*. Ramona had put on a dressing gown and was again watching the promotional video that featured her, but now she wasn't crying. On the coffee table in front of her were two bowls of cookie dough ice cream.

Blackmoor put on his underpants and sat next to her on the sofa.

"Have some ice cream and celebrate my birthday with me," she said.

Blackmoor generally avoided foods that were high in sugar, but as it was Ramona's birthday, he thought he'd indulge himself and picked up a bowl of ice cream and started eating.

"Best birthday ever!" she exclaimed.

Chapter Sixteen

Toby had phoned Blackmoor and asked if he would help him with a man called Clinton O'Shaughnessy who was suffering from PTSD (post-traumatic stress disorder). O'Shaughnessy had been living at a homeless shelter and had been rushed to an accident and emergency department after he had tried to commit suicide by taking a drug overdose. After the medical staff at the accident and emergency department had pumped out O'Shaughnessy's stomach and saved his life, they had transferred him to a psychiatric ward, but now the staff on the psychiatric ward were saying he was ready for discharge and had asked Toby to pick him up and return him to the homeless shelter. They were offering no follow-up care and Toby had asked Blackmoor to assess and treat O'Shaughnessy.

Blackmoor said he'd review the case but added he was a psychiatrist and not a miracle worker.

Toby had picked up Blackmoor on the way to the hospital and while they were in the car, Blackmoor read O'Shaughnessy's case history, which Toby had downloaded to a laptop computer.

O'Shaughnessy had been a first lieutenant in the Marine Corps, had seen action in the Congo, and was suffering from PTSD as a result of the things he'd seen and done in combat. On his return to the United States, O'Shaughnessy had tried to hang himself but had been cut down before he had choked to death. He had been discharged from the armed forces after receiving psychiatric care, which included counselling, group therapy, and chemotherapy. In the ten years since then, he had been prescribed an assortment of antidepressants and tranquilisers, he had had repeated admissions to hospitals, he had used alcohol to blank out the bad memories, and he had tried to commit suicide another three times.

"I contacted the Marine Corps and they said O'Shaughnessy is now a civilian and they have no further obligation to take care of him," Toby said. "His parents are still living and I phoned his father who said his son never came back from Africa and he doesn't want to be contacted about him anymore. O'Shaughnessy has a younger sister, who is now married with kids, and when I phoned her, she said when her brother eventually dies, by suicide or for any other reason, she doesn't want to be informed."

"Everyone has given up on him," Blackmoor said. "Except you."

When they arrived at the psychiatric ward, the nursing staff immediately recognised Blackmoor and were visibly surprised that the famous Dr Dominic Blackmoor had come to pick up O'Shaughnessy. Blackmoor asked if he could talk to O'Shaughnessy privately before they took him back to the homeless shelter and the ward sister said he could use the doctor's office. She sent one of her nurses to fetch O'Shaughnessy and escorted Blackmoor to the doctors' office herself.

When Blackmoor saw O'Shaughnessy, he was shocked. In the one and only picture Blackmoor had seen of him, which was in the short case summary Toby had downloaded, O'Shaughnessy was a handsome athletically built young man in his Marine Corps parade dress uniform, but, although he was still only in his mid-thirties, he looked to be in his mid-sixties and was as emaciated as a Nazi concentration camp survivor. Years of alcohol abuse, malnutrition, and self-neglect had aged him.

"I'm Dr Dominic Blackmoor," he said on meeting O'Shaughnessy.

"I know who you are," O'Shaughnessy replied. "A lot of people at the homeless shelter said you were a friend of Toby's, but I didn't know if it was true or just claptrap."

"What happened to you?" Blackmoor asked as soon as they were alone and sitting down.

"All I ever wanted was to be a marine, and as soon as I was old enough, I joined the Marine Corps," O'Shaughnessy replied.

"My father had never been in the military but I had a football coach who was a former marine and he said, 'When you go on your honeymoon with the woman you want to spend the rest of your life with, you'll be happier than you thought was possible. And when the woman you love gives you children, you'll be even happier. But what's best in life is going off to war with your brothers-in-arms.' And he was right! Have you ever experienced that yourself?"

"No," Blackmoor said. "I've heard many people say that marching off to war with your comrades-in-arms is an incredible thrill, but I've never personally experienced it."

"My company was posted to the Congo Basin," O'Shaughnessy continued. "We were supporting the standing government's forces who were suppressing an insurrection, and we had all the problems the American forces had in Vietnam in the 1960s. We were unable to close with the enemy and we kept losing men to land mines, booby traps, and snipers. And the rebels would kidnap children and force them to be soldiers, and on the rare occasions we could get close enough to return fire, we were forced to shoot kids because they were shooting at us."

Blackmoor had followed the campaign on the news as it had taken place and he had heard reports that war crimes had been perpetrated by both sides, including the torture and execution of captured enemy combatants, but he had also heard that the rebels frequently and routinely committed crimes against humanity, unlike the standing government's forces and the American troops who were supporting them. As a British investigative reporter had defined it: "The Americans were backing the *Good Guys* against the *Bad Guys*." And the democratically elected government had the support of the vast majority of the indigenous population, which was the main reason the insurrection was crushed in under a year.

In reference to the atrocities committed by American and allied troops during the campaign, one military historian had suggested that if the torture of a captured enemy soldier could glean intel that could win battles or save lives, it could be deemed to be a lesser of evils, and if enemy combatants were captured and the troops who had captured them didn't have the facilities to guard them, to execute them in the field could be regarded as a military necessity. Blackmoor strongly disagreed and did not condone the torture or execution of captured enemy combatants under any circumstances.

"The snipers targeted officers, and when our company captain was killed, I was promoted from the second lieutenant to first lieutenant and placed in charge of the company," O'Shaughnessy said. "It hurt when an officer, who was also a friend, was killed in action, but I can't describe the frustration, pain, and anger I felt when one of the men under my command, who I was responsible for, was killed. And every time I lost a man, my hatred for the enemy grew. Then military intelligence learnt that a notorious rebel leader called Damien Nkulu was regrouping his forces at the village where he was born and raised. We were ordered to engage Nkulu's warband and we launched a surprise attack in tilt-rotor aircraft."

A tilt-rotor aircraft has the body and wings of an airplane but helicopter rotor blades are mounted on top of each wing, enabling it to take off and land vertically and giving it the manoeuvrability and hovering capability of a helicopter. Once in the air, the rotor blades and the engines that powered them could tilt forwards and the aircraft then resembles a twin-engine airplane, giving it the high speed, long-range, and high-altitude cruise capability of an airplane.

"But when we arrived at Nkulu's village, there were no troops there, just unarmed civilians, and most of them were women, children, and the elderly," O'Shaughnessy said. "It was partly the adrenaline-fuelled expectation of going into battle, it was partly the frustration of having lost comrades and of being unable to engage the enemy, it was partly because we'd become accustomed to fighting civilians who didn't look like soldiers but who were carrying guns or setting booby traps, and it was partly the pure hatred we felt for the enemy, but we slaughtered everyone in the village: about four hundred people. And we didn't just shoot them, some were bayoneted, and some of the young girls were gang raped before they had their throats cut. I always led by example and from the front, and I shot thirty-one people myself, but as the officer in command, I'm responsible for all four hundred murders."

Blackmoor was both horror-struck and disgusted, and in any other context he would have said so, but as O'Shaughnessy's psychotherapist, he maintained a non-judgemental demeanour.

"You authored a beginner's guide to psychology called *If It Makes Sense to You*, in which you covered *hate crimes* and *war crimes* and explained why ordinary people who have never committed a violent or antisocial act before can suddenly become sadistic psychopaths, and quite a few therapists have brought that section of your book to my attention," O'Shaughnessy said.

The section of the book O'Shaughnessy was referring to read:

Much of human behaviour stems from our hunting ape ancestors, in the same way that much of the behaviour of the domestic dog derives from the wolf pack, and it was essential that our ape men ancestors, who hunted in packs, cooperated, and to facilitate group collaboration, they evolved the capacity to learn codes of conduct and morality towards each other. It was equally as important that if they came into conflict with rival packs of hunting apes, and were competing for resources, that the codes of conduct and morality they felt for each other, did not apply to other packs of hunting apes and they could harm, rob, and kill them without qualms.

The desire to make war on other packs, tribes, nations, or peoples, and invent more efficient weapons to be able to do so, was probably the driving force that took our ancestors from the Stone Age to the Bronze Age, and from the Bronze Age to the Iron Age, and so on to the present day. And throughout history, the success of any civilisation has been measured by its ability to militarily dominate other peoples.

The desire to make war on rival peoples is one of our basic drives and if we can define someone as Other, either for race, religion, politics, or for any other reason, the codes of conduct and morality that apply to our own people will not apply to them and we can harm them or kill them with no feelings of guilt for doing so.

"I've experienced believing a group of people to be *Other* and of feeling no immediate guilt for killing them," O'Shaughnessy said. "Have you?"

"No," Blackmoor replied. "I've researched the subject in depth but that's also something I've never personally experienced."

"After the massacre, some of our superior officers wanted to court martial us for war crimes and some of them wanted to cover up the mass slaughter to prevent an international incident," O'Shaughnessy said. "While they were deciding what to do with us, my company was posted to a small ghost town that was deep in hostile territory. About half of the buildings had been shelled to rubble and the town's inhabitants had either fled or had been evacuated and we sheltered in the buildings that were still standing.

Six days after we had been stationed at the ghost town, Nkulu mustered all the troops at his disposal and attacked my company.

It never occurred to me until much later, but perhaps we had been put there as bait to draw Nkulu into a set-piece battle, or possibly we had been posted there so we'd all be killed and the problem of what to do with us would go away, or maybe we had been stationed there for both reasons.

There were ninety-eight of us left by then and Nkulu had marshalled over five hundred men.

We fought Nkulu's forces through the rubble of the town street by street, house by house, even room by room. We were trained and equipped for that type of battle, whereas Nkulu and his warband were hit-and-run jungle guerrillas, and we killed two or three of them for every one of us they killed, but as he had us outnumbered better

The Spectre

than five-to-one, he could take the loses and still win the battle, and he wanted us all dead because of what we had done at his village.

Throughout the battle, I had repeatedly ordered my radio operator to request reinforcements – which never came – but once what was left of my decimated company was completely surrounded and we were defending a single building, I ordered my radio operator to request a missile strike on our own position. The missiles came quickly enough and Nkulu and most of his men were killed in the strike.

After the missile strike, there were only six members of my company still alive, but dead or alive, we were all heroes, and I was awarded a Silver Star for my part in the battle.

History is written by the winners and the massacre at Nkulu's village wasn't covered up, it was just forgotten.

I can't forget about the four hundred people I murdered and I can't forgive myself for killing them."

Blackmoor studied O'Shaughnessy's facial expressions, speech patterns, and body language, and he noticed no self-pity in O'Shaughnessy's demeanour, just guilt.

"You owe the world four hundred lives," Blackmoor said. "You need to do as much good as you have harm to even the score."

O'Shaughnessy was visibly surprised by Blackmoor's proposal and it was obviously the first time anyone had ever suggested it to him.

"I'm a former marine; that was all I ever wanted to be," O'Shaughnessy replied. "All I know about is killing."

"You can find a way," Blackmoor said. "There are surgeons and there are stretcher-bearers. You can help with the homeless, as does Toby. There are several charitable organisations that raise money by selling donated goods and you could do voluntary work at a thrift store. Ten dollars can save a life in a poverty-stricken nation and you could get a job and donate money to a famine relief charity."

"Are you trying to tell me if I donate four thousand dollars to charity that will make up for the four hundred lives I've taken?" O'Shaughnessy quickly replied.

"No," Blackmoor said. "Ten dollars can pay for food that feeds a child for one day. If you kill a child, you've taken many days – many years – away from that child. You could spend the rest of your life trying to make up for the harm you've done and never even the score."

O'Shaughnessy cogitated on Blackmoor's advice.

Blackmoor sat in silence and gave O'Shaughnessy time to mull over what had been said and after about ten minutes of deep thought, O'Shaughnessy responded: "Okay, I'll give it a try."

Chapter Seventeen

As Blackmoor had gone to Vikki's apartment straight from work, he showered before they engaged in a sex game. After showering, he went to her living room wearing only a bathrobe, and as soon as he'd sat down on her couch, she came out of her bedroom. Vikki was naked and the sex game she had opted to play was *The Irresistible Temptress*. She had a variety of erotic lingerie that she could have worn while playing *The Irresistible Temptress* but, on this occasion, she had chosen to be completely nude.

Vikki sauntered over to Blackmoor and laid across his lap with her naked torso against his bare thighs. He started to give her a massage that alternated from hard, soft, and tickly in random order and ranged from the back of her neck to the backs of her thighs, and every so often, he'd reach between her legs and stroke her vagina.

"If God made anything sexier than your body, he kept it for himself," Blackmoor said. For Vikki, compliments were an essential component of the game.

"Give me some love pats," Vikki said after about fifteen minutes of being massaged. While she was playing *The Irresistible Temptress*, they never needed to use safe words and she would simply tell Blackmoor what she wanted him to do to her.

Blackmoor started gently patting her on alternate butt cheeks.

"Spank me harder," Vikki eventually said.

Blackmoor made the spanking a tad harder and left longer periods of time between smacks to allow her to fully luxuriate in the sting.

Blackmoor intensified the spanking twice, at Vikki's request, and as the smacks became harder, she wriggled and squealed with delight.

"Make love to me now," Vikki said when she felt the spanking had reached a crescendo.

Sometimes Vikki liked his love making to be romantic and gentle and at other times she liked it passionate and rough, and from the words she'd used, her tone of voice, and previous experience, Blackmoor knew that Vikki wanted the sex to be romantic and gentle.

She got up from across his knees, sat on his lap, and they started kissing.

When Blackmoor thought the time was right, he picked her up, carried her to her bedroom, and gently set her down on her bed. He was still wearing a bathrobe and he let it drop to the floor before joining Vikki on the bed to make love to her.

Chapter Eighteen

ATF Special Agents Iain McNaughton and Cheryl Koenig had driven to a shooting club that was owned by a retired ATF Special Agent called Jake Schapiro. Schapiro first and foremost taught civilians, and it was Schapiro who had given Blackmoor most of his formal instruction when he had wanted a permit to carry a pistol, but he closed his shooting club to the public one Sunday a month so he and the people he employed as instructors could hone their skills.

Iain and Cheryl had served with Schapiro in the ATF, and as they had been comrades-in-arms, Schapiro had invited them to participate in his monthly training sessions.

The club had a gymnasium where students were taught the basic manoeuvres with replica pistols, a fixed target range, an assault course range, and a dark room as many gunfights take place at night and indoors and combatants need to learn to locate and shoot an enemy by using their ears and by the light of the muzzle flashes.

Iain used the restroom before he followed Cheryl into the heart of the building and when he arrived at the gymnasium, he saw Cheryl was bound to a chair and a ball gag had been stuffed into her mouth. A man wearing a tight leather hooded mask that resembled a Mexican wrestler's mask was standing behind her and was holding a gun to her head. Lying on the floor were the dead bodies of Jake Schapiro and six of his staff and written on the wall in their blood were the words:

"BE AFRAID!

BE VERY AFRAID!"

Iain knew it was *The Spectre* and that he'd soon be fighting for his life as well as for Cheryl's.

"Drop your sidearm!" *The Spectre* instructed.

Iain unfastened his belt buckle and let his gun belt and pistol fall to the floor. He then walked slowly across the gymnasium towards *The Spectre* and sized him up as he closed with him. *The Spectre* was about five feet nine inches tall and Iain was about seven inches taller and twenty pounds heavier. When they were about twenty paces away from each other, *The Spectre* placed his pistol on the floor and walked towards Iain. While serving as a Green Beret, Iain had killed a few men with his bare hands and was confident he could defeat his smaller opponent.

Suddenly, Iain lunged at *The Spectre* with a combination of karate kicks and punches. He attacked from a standing position, and not from a guard stance, giving him the element of surprise, and all the techniques he employed were deathblows. *The Spectre* blocked or evaded all of Iain's kicks and punches and concluded their initial engagement by knocking Iain to the floor with a palm heel technique to his forehead.

Iain was knocked dizzy and was defenceless but *The Spectre* was toying with him and gave him time to recover.

The Spectre had superhuman speed and strength and as Iain got to his feet, he recalled a few previous occasions when he'd encountered men with such herculean capabilities: when he was a Green Beret, Iain had been posted deep behind enemy lines to train native guerrilla forces and had often liaised with deep penetration para commando units like the Navy SEALs who were sent to perform exigent operations, which were usually sabotage missions but were occasionally assassination or rescue missions. Just before they went into action, the commandos would swallow some tablets that gave them superhuman reflexes, speed, and strength and made them chemically enhanced super soldiers. The tablets were only issued to elite commando units whose missions would only take a few hours, as the stimulants were only effective for two to three hours and most soldiers are in combat for weeks or even months. Iain guessed that although *The Spectre* was highly trained in unarmed combat, he had probably taken military grade stimulants.

Iain had fallen near the dead bodies of Schapiro and his six instructors and as he got to his feet, he noticed that one of Schapiro's men was wearing a knife on his belt. It was a black Fairbairn-Sykes British commando knife with a double-edged seven-inch-long blade and Iain drew the knife from its scabbard and walked towards *The Spectre*. *The Spectre* had seen Iain draw the knife, and he could have picked up his pistol, but he was enjoying the sport.

Iain had sparred with many people with rubber knives and he very rarely lost a knife fight. He frequently sparred with people when his opponents were unarmed and he was wielding a rubber knife and, in that context, he had never lost a bout to anyone, including Blackmoor, Marty, or any of the international martial arts experts who had visited Blackmoor's club.

When Cheryl saw *The Spectre* was going to engage Iain with his bare hands when Iain was armed with a knife, she knew *The Spectre* was a dead man.

Iain thrust and slashed at *The Spectre* but *The Spectre* dodged or parried all of Iain's techniques. Iain gathered *The Spectre* was still toying with him but, in doing so, was focusing his full attention on the knife blade. Iain exploited his opponent's overconfidence and inattentional blindness and attacked with a kick to *The Spectre's* midsection. The kick sent *The Spectre* staggering backwards and while he was off balance, Iain lunged forwards to drive his blade through *The Spectre's* right eye and into his brain: an instant kill. *The Spectre* barely evaded the thrust and the razor-sharp edge of the knife cut through his mask and gave him a deep gash along the right side of his head. As *The Spectre* dodged the knife, he grabbed Iain's right wrist with his right hand and slammed his left forearm into Iain's right elbow. There was a crunching of bone as Iain's right elbow was bent against the joint and fractured. Iain screamed in pain as *The Spectre* broke his arm and threw him to the floor.

The Spectre picked up the commando knife and he and Iain stared at each other. The blood from the deep gash on the right side of *The Spectre's* head was running down his face and he had come within an inch of death; *The Spectre* was experiencing an adrenaline rush.

Then, much to Iain's surprise, *The Spectre* threw the knife to him. Iain clumsily got to his feet and picked up the knife with his left hand. Iain walked towards *The Spectre* and when he was within a few feet of him, he drew back his hand and threw the knife with all his might at *The Spectre's* chest. *The Spectre* was taken by surprise but was able to twist his body and evade the knife, which stuck into the wall behind him. Iain charged forwards to drive his fingers into *The Spectre's* eyes but *The Spectre* seized Iain's left wrist and broke his left elbow the same way he'd broken his right elbow. Without a pause, *The Spectre* stamped on Iain's left knee and broke his leg at the knee joint. Iain screamed as he collapsed to the floor in agony.

Now *The Spectre* had broken both of Iain's arms and one of his legs, he could focus his attention on Cheryl. The gymnasium was quite austere and had little to tie her to other than a chair but he intended to use his imagination. He planned to remove the ball gag before he went to work on her as he wanted to hear her try to negotiate for her life at the beginning of the sex game and beg for death towards the end.

Three hours later, he'd finished. Cheryl was naked, bound in a hogtie position with her wrists and ankles behind her back, and had suffocated to death with a plastic bag over her head.

Iain was still conscious and had tried to slowly crawl across the gymnasium to get to his gun belt. He was hoping that even with two broken arms, he could point and fire his pistol.

The Spectre had cleaned up the crime scene, leaving no clue as to his identity, and just before he left, he removed his mask, got down on one knee beside Iain, and rolled him onto his side so they could look at each other's faces. Iain's expression of agony changed to one of complete surprise and alarm when he recognised *The Spectre* and realised who he was. *The Spectre* had done this as his final act of sadistic cruelty. *The Spectre* then grabbed Iain's head with both hands and broke his neck. For dramatic flourish, *The Spectre* gave Iain's head an extra twist, so it was turned 180 degrees and facing backwards.

Chapter Nineteen

The night cleaner arrived at Schapiro's shooting club at 8.45 pm. He was a little surprised to see several vehicles in the car park at that time of night but he wasn't alarmed and went into the shooting club. He soon found the dead bodies of Iain, Cheryl, Schapiro, and Schapiro's six instructors and as he ran to the exit, he called the police with his smartphone. The police arrived within minutes and immediately summoned the coroner and the crime scene investigators. It was obvious that *The Spectre* had committed the murders and the police also called FBI Supervisory Special Agent Ramona Cortez and her task force.

When Cortez learnt that two of the victims were close friends of Blackmoor, she informed him of the murders personally and before he could hear about them from anybody else.

Blackmoor felt a level of anguish he had never experienced before. He had always been fascinated, intrigued, and even sexually aroused by sadistic murders but this was the first-time people close to him had been tortured and slain. Blackmoor had counselled many people who had experienced psychological trauma as a result of contact with killers but he'd never really understood the pain they were going through until now. Blackmoor had prescribed sedatives and tranquillisers for many of the people he had treated and he considered using pharmaceuticals to numb the pain he was experiencing but he needed to keep his mind clear to hunt down *The Spectre*.

Blackmoor confided his thoughts and feelings to Toby and likened himself to a consultant psychiatrist he'd known called Dr. Douglas Wallace. Dr. Douglas Wallace was a specialist in drug and alcohol addiction who, as a result of a painful knee injury, became addicted to morphine. Once cured of his addiction, he frequently stated that he didn't have a full understanding of drug dependency until he became a morphine addict himself.

Toby said he was going to put the images out of his mind, as he had done when he was an army combat medic and had witnessed horrendous injuries and inhumane atrocities. Blackmoor considered trying to ring-fence his emotions, as had Toby, but he wanted to get into *The Spectre's* head, and he wouldn't be able to do so if he went into denial about some of the murders *The Spectre* had committed.

Blackmoor knew he'd be unable to function normally and he referred all of his patients to other psychiatrists, he told Marty that he'd have to run the self-defence club alone, and he cancelled all of his social engagements.

Blackmoor visited the crime scene where Iain and Cheryl had been tortured to death but he couldn't bring himself to be present at their autopsies. He read the autopsy reports but was unable to glean any new insights and the reports only confirmed the offender profile he had already formulated. Blackmoor spent two weeks reviewing every piece of information that had been collected about *The Spectre* but he couldn't get any closer to him.

As he hadn't left his home for a fortnight, Blackmoor thought a change of surroundings might clear his head and he went to a boxing gym to work off his anger and frustration on a punching bag. The gym was owned and managed by an African American called Peter Moray, who had been both an Olympic and a professional boxer and was the man Blackmoor had approached when he had wanted to learn how to box.

The gym was quite crowded and pugilists were skipping, shadow boxing, working out on punch bags, or doing callisthenics. At the heart of the gym was a boxing ring and Joe Morgan, one of Moray's assistant coaches, was in the ring, coaching a promising young welterweight. Morgan had been a professional heavyweight boxer and Blackmoor had learnt even more about boxing from Morgan than he had from Moray. Morgan was wearing a padded chest and belly protector and a pair of padded training mitts and the agile young welterweight was moving around Morgan, punching the body protector and the padded mitts.

Blackmoor had put on a pair of boxing gloves to protect his knuckles and as soon as a punching bag became available, he started pounding on it. Every so often, he'd kick the punch bag or practise another oriental martial arts technique, which drew some surprised glances from a few of the pugilists but most of them were too involved in their own workouts to notice anything Blackmoor did.

Once the welterweight had finished his workout, Morgan invited Blackmoor to train with him in the boxing ring. Blackmoor climbed into the ring and started punching the padded mitts and body protector Morgan was wearing. While he was doing so, Morgan gave Blackmoor both negative and positive feedback about his boxing techniques.

Blackmoor became more and more involved in the cathartic aspect of an aggressive workout as his caged emotions had found an outlet. The anger Blackmoor felt about two of his closest friends being tortured to death and the frustration he felt because he couldn't catch their killer was clouding his mind and he was becoming increasingly oblivious to his surroundings.

Suddenly, Blackmoor spun on the spot and struck Morgan in the chest with a back kick. The padded chest and belly protector ensured Morgan wasn't injured, but the powerful kick sent the much larger man staggering backwards onto the ropes. Blackmoor continued his onslaught and pounded on the mitts and the body protector while Morgan leaned against the ropes and held his hands up to protect his face.

"Blackmoor!" Moray yelled across the gym.

Blackmoor was yanked back to reality. He looked around and saw everyone in the gym had stopped their endeavours and were staring at him in opened-mouthed disbelief. Blackmoor took a step back and bowed to Morgan. Although the gesture was from the oriental martial arts, he hoped Morgan and everyone else at the gym would understand it was both an apology and a mark of respect.

Chapter Twenty

Richard Clack had applied to join every branch of the armed forces, every law enforcement agency, and every private security firm in America but had been rejected as he had asthma and epilepsy, both of which were controlled with medication. He had worked as a sales assistant in a fishing and outdoors equipment store and had learnt enough about the merchandise he was selling to get a job as a tour guide in the California forests and would escort tourists on nature rambles, fishing trips, and camping holidays.

Clack was a pathological liar with a vivid imagination and would tell tall tales that he'd been a Navy SEAL, a bounty hunter, a scout-sniper, a big game hunter, a CIA agent, and a bodyguard for the rich and famous, but his favourite fantasy was he'd been an FBI Special Agent in the Behavioural Analysis Unit and had hunted serial killers.

Clack had a fascination for serial killers, as well as for the people who hunt them down, and he'd developed a particular interest in *The Spectre*. He'd learnt by reading Blackmoor's offender profile that *The Spectre* preyed on physically powerful men who were partnered with very beautiful women and Clack tried to predict who *The Spectre's* next victims would be. He studied the media and concluded likely targets for *The Spectre* were Vanessa Lundy and Hank Murphy.

Vanessa Lundy arranged sex and fetish parties for the rich, the famous, and the powerful and Hank Murphy was her head of security.

Lundy hosted sex and fetish parties at her Los Angeles mansion, which was popularly nicknamed *The Sex Palace*, and most of her clientele paid her to take part in orgies or for partner swapping, but Lundy was a licenced sex worker and a trained dominatrix and her patrons could indulge in a broad spectrum of fetishes including voyeurism, exhibitionism, BDSM, uniforms, leather, rubber, or anything else that took their fancy.

Her mansion was decorated like a billionaire's home, and not like a bordello or a place of business, as Lundy wanted her clientele to feel like guests and not like paying customers.

Lundy greeted her patrons in the main hall of her mansion and at the end of the main hall was a platform were girls performed strip tease or pole dances throughout her parties. Several of the bedrooms were furnished with giant size beds but Lundy had found that no matter how big the beds were, someone always fell off the edge in the throng, and in response she had converted one of the larger downstairs rooms to an *Orgy Room*. The floor of the *Orgy Room* had been covered from wall to wall in extra thick foam mats and many large pillows had been scattered on the cushioned flooring.

Although the *Orgy Room* was the room that saw the most action, in the basement of the mansion were two S&M dungeons. One of the dungeons was as clean, polished, and well-lit as an operating theatre, and the other was decorated like a Dark Age torture chamber.

Hank Murphy had been a sergeant in the military police and after leaving the army had worked as a security guard at a Las Vegas casino. Lundy had hired him to work as a doorman at her parties but as her parties started to attract the rich, the famous, and the powerful, she had to employ additional security guards to ensure her clients' safety and privacy and Murphy had progressed from being her bouncer to being her head of security.

Clack had emailed Lundy and had warned her *The Spectre* might be coming after her and had offered her his services as a bodyguard. Lundy received no end of crank emails but she had brought Clack's email to Murphy's attention and he had brought it to the attention of the police. A couple of police officers in *The Spectre* task force had questioned Clack but decided he wasn't a serious suspect and had no connection to, or knowledge of, *The Spectre*.

The Spectre

Clack revelled in the attention he'd received as a consequence of being briefly involved in *The Spectre* investigation and he became fascinated with the scenario of shooting *The Spectre* and saving Lundy's life. He gleaned a colossal amount of information about Lundy from the internet and for a few weeks he conducted surveillance of her sex and fetish parties with night vision binoculars.

While Clack was trying to predict how *The Spectre* would conduct an attack on Lundy and Murphy, an idea occurred to him: if he couldn't catch *The Spectre*, he could become a rival to him.

One evening, Clack surveilled Lundy's place of business and observed that forty-seven people were at her mansion: Lundy and Murphy, thirty-four clients, an additional security guard, a chef, a barman (or mixologist as he preferred to be called), and eight sex workers who Lundy had employed as ushers, waitresses, strip tease dancers, pole dancers, lap dancers, or prostitutes, depending on what her patrons wanted and were willing to pay for.

Clack had put on a black hooded tracksuit and had selected the equipment he thought he'd need, most of which he'd packed in a backpack. His primary weapons were two 9mm semi-automatic pistols, which he carried in fast-draw holsters like a Wild West gunslinger. Clack had fitted his pistols with silencers and long ammunition magazines, enabling each pistol to hold thirty-three rounds.

Clack stealthily approached the mansion's front entrance via the car parking area, using the parked vehicles for cover. As many of the people who came to Lundy's parties wanted discretion, there were no CCTV cameras and Clack could get near the mansion without being seen. Murphy's additional security guard was stationed at the front door and as soon as Clack was close enough, he shot the security guard through the head. The security guard was dead before he could raise the alarm and Clack stepped over his dead body and entered the mansion.

Once inside, he took a tranquilliser gun from his backpack and started hunting for Murphy. Clack had learnt from information he'd gleaned via the internet that during the parties, Murphy usually waited in Lundy's administration office unless an unwanted caller wouldn't go away or a client became troublesome and needed to be escorted off the premises.

On reaching Lundy's administration office, Clack charged through the open doorway and shot Murphy with the tranquiliser gun. Murphy was reading current news articles on his tablet, and he tried to get up from his chair with the tranquiliser dart stuck in his chest, but he quickly lost consciousness and collapsed to the floor.

Clack pulled the dart from Murphy's chest and returned the dart and the tranquilliser gun to his backpack. He then drew an electroshock stun gun from his pocket and walked to the huge main hall of the mansion. As the night was still young, the sex games hadn't started yet, and Lundy and her patrons were still chatting. One of the sex workers was performing a pole dance on the platform and the other seven sex workers were wearing French maids' costumes and were serving drinks and snacks that had been prepared by the chef and the barman.

Then Clack saw Lundy. She occasionally joined in the sex parties if she was paid to do so or if a very attractive customer, either male or female, had taken her fancy, but even when she wasn't partying, she often wore a fetish costume to make her clients feel she was part of the festivities and not just overseeing. She had a variety of costumes including a dominatrix, a French maid, a schoolmistress, and a schoolgirl, but as the current event had the ambience of a cocktail party, she was wearing a long evening dress and a sapphire blue tiara with a matching necklace and matching earrings.

Clack walked towards Lundy as the electroshock weapon he was armed with administered a shock through direct contact and he had to be within arm's reach to stun her with it. As soon as he was close enough, he shocked her. Lundy started convulsing and collapsed to the floor. She was fully aware of her surrounding but had no control of her body and was helpless.

Clack put the stun gun back in his pocket, drew his pistols, and started shooting Lundy's patrons. As his pistols were fitted with silencers, he'd shot seven people before everyone at the party became aware they were being fired on.

Most of the women started frantically screaming and everyone who hadn't been shot ran towards a doorway at the back of the hall that led to the *Orgy Room*. Clack fired on them as they converged on the exit and in the crush some of his bullets went through two, three, or four people.

The chef and the barman heard the screaming and ran to the main hall to investigate, and Clack shot them both.

One of Lundy's sex workers was carrying a smartphone, which she snatched from her pocket as she ran towards the exit. She dialled 9-1-1 and the emergency services telephonist soon responded: "9-1-1, what's your emergency?"

The attractive young sex worker was just about to call for help, when a bullet hit her in the back. As she fell, she dropped her smartphone and it slid across the floor.

The details of the owner of the smartphone and its location automatically came up on the emergency services telephonist's computer screen and she saw the owner of the smartphone was Caroline Lopez, a licensed sex worker, and see was calling from the mansion where Vanessa Lundy hosted her sex and fetish parties. The telephonist assumed that Caroline Lopez had the emergency number on the speed dial and had accidentally pressed the speed dial button and was unaware she had done so. The telephonist could hear some activity but assumed it was Lundy's clientele partying.

Clack pursued the fleeing people into the *Orgy Room*, many of whom were wounded, and as there was no exit from the room and little to hide behind, Clack picked off the survivors with ease.

Once everyone was dead or incapacitated, Clack walked around the mansion, counting the bodies and finishing off the wounded with headshots. Clack was aware that forty-seven people were currently at the mansion, and once he'd accounted for all of them, he focused his attention on Lundy. He picked her up, carried her to one of the ground floor bedrooms, and laid her face down on the bed. Clack tied her wrists and ankles to the bedposts in a spread-eagle position with ropes he'd brought for that purpose and he gagged her with two bandanas: one he forced into her mouth, the other he tied around her face to stop her spitting out the first. He then took a large Bowie knife from his backpack and started to cut away Lundy's clothes. The Bowie knife had an eleven-inch blade and a razor-sharp edge and he could cut away her clothing with little effort. She was soon naked except for a pair of stockings and a suspender belt, which he decided not to cut off as they looked erotic and wouldn't get in his way.

Clack had brought a tube of lipstick with which he wrote on the wall:

"BE AFRAID!

BE VERY AFRAID!"

He then went to fetch Murphy. Murphy was a big man and Clack was unable to carry him and had to drag him to the bedroom. Once there, Clack sat astride Murphy's chest and punched him in the face with all his strength. Clack punched the unconscious man another three times to create the illusion he'd overpowered Murphy mano-a-mano.

Clack then took a sturdy leather belt from his backpack and used it to lash Lundy across her buttocks. The effects of the electroshock weapon had worn off and she involuntarily cried out but the gag muffled her screams.

The lashing continued and Lundy twisted and struggled to dodge the belt as best as she could with the little slack that was in the ropes.

Clack ogled Lundy as she struggled and screamed and as red welts crisscrossed her butt.

When Clack had shot the security guard at the front door, it was the most intense thrill he had ever experienced in his entire life. The evening had got progressively better since then and beating Lundy was the biggest thrill so far.

The emergency services telephonist continued to listen in on Caroline Lopez's smartphone out of curiosity more than concern and she eventually decided a solution to her dilemma would be to send a police car to Lundy's mansion to inform Caroline Lopez she had accidentally contacted the emergency services. It would make the police look efficient but not draw unnecessary attention to Lundy's sex and fetish parties or cause any embarrassment to the rich, famous, and influential people who go to them. The two police officers the telephonist directed to Lundy's mansion were Eric Wilson and Virginia Wren but she told them it wasn't an emergency and not to use their flashing lights or sirens.

Clack wanted to turn Lundy onto her back to rape her and he stunned her again with his electroshock weapon to render her helpless so that he could reposition her without a struggle.

Officers Eric Wilson and Virginia Wren arrived at Lundy's mansion and found the dead body of the security guard at the front entrance. After calling for backup, they cautiously entered the mansion. When they saw the main hall and about thirty dead bodies, they suspected terrorists were responsible as that level of carnage seemed excessive for armed robbers or an individual gunman.

Once he'd repositioned Lundy, Clack took his clothes off and was naked except for a pair of black socks. He was just about to climb onto the bed to rape Lundy when Wilson and Wren entered the room with their pistols drawn. Wilson and Wren had no way of knowing if Clack was one of the gunmen who'd shot Lundy's staff and clients or if he was one of Lundy's customers who'd hidden until after the gunmen had left, but as he was naked except for a pair of black socks, the latter option seemed to be the most likely.

After a moment of surprised indecision, Clack lunged for his guns, which he'd placed on the floor next to his clothes. As he bent over to pick up his pistols, Wren drew and fired her taser. Her taser fired two long wires that were tipped with barbed electrodes, which harpooned Clack's left buttock. As the shock from her taser went through his body, he started convulsing and fired a single shot from each of his pistols before falling to the floor.

Chapter Twenty-One

Richard Clack was escorted to a police station, the paramedics took Vanessa Lundy and Hank Murphy to a hospital, and the dead bodies were transported to the coroner's facility for autopsy. Clack confessed to being *The Spectre* as soon as he was questioned and Ramona Cortez was informed of his arrest and confession.

Cortez interviewed Clack and he convinced her and everyone else on her task force that he was *The Spectre*.

Cortez arranged a press conference to announce that a suspect was in custody and she informed Blackmoor that *The Spectre* had been captured. Blackmoor asked to see the recording of her interview with Richard Clack and after studying it intently, he requested to speak to Cortez privately.

"It's not him!" Blackmoor said as soon as they were alone. "He's a copycat killer."

"He knows every minute detail of the case," Cortez replied. "And he was caught while beating and raping an attractive woman after he'd shot to death forty-five people, and forty-five dead bodies are compelling evidence."

"Very few details of the case have been kept secret," Blackmoor said. "He could have learnt everything he knows about *The Spectre* on the internet and there's no physical evidence connecting Clack to the other murders."

"The only physical evidence left by *The Spectre* are the slugs and spent cartridge cases from a 7.5mm Caledfwlch Assault Carbine and a 9mm semi-automatic pistol," Cortez replied. "And Clack said he had obtained both weapons on the black market and had thrown them into the sea after he'd learnt that the police had identified them as the weapons he was using."

Shortly after speaking to Blackmoor, Cortez held a press conference in a very crowded hall and announced a suspect had been arrested and was being prosecuted for *The Spectre* homicides.

"Richard Clack is nothing like the offender profile conceived by Dr. Dominic Blackmoor," one of the journalists said.

"That was a mistake I think we all made," Cortez replied. "We were looking for an evil genius or a hulking brute, and when you're looking for a serial killer, generally speaking, you don't look for Baron Frankenstein or his monster, you look for a little man; the vast majority of serial killers are inconspicuous little men."

Blackmoor decided to leave the building before any journalists had spotted him and discreetly entered an elevator. As the elevator doors were closing, Wayne McLintock quickly rushed in.

"Did you know that Napoleon won more battles than Alexander the Great, Julius Caesar, and Hannibal the Annihilator put together, but he's mostly remembered for Waterloo: the one battle he lost," McLintock said.

Blackmoor responded with a puzzled facial expression as he couldn't understand the relevance of McLintock's comment.

"I've solved more crimes and arrested more criminals than any other three law enforcement officers you could think of put together, but the one case I'm remembered for is *The Elfin Forest Killer* investigation," McLintock added.

Blackmoor then understood that McLintock was comparing himself to Napoleon and stating *The Elfin Forest Killer* investigation was his Waterloo. *The Elfin Forest Killer* abducted women and kept them as sex toys for a time before he murdered them and dumped their bodies in the Elfin Forest. McLintock was put in charge of the investigation but he wouldn't allow his task force to consult profilers as he believed offender profiling was nonsense. McLintock and his task force had spent months trying to apprehend *The Elfin Forest*

Killer without success and in desperation McLintock's superiors had ordered him to allow Blackmoor to take part in the investigation, and Blackmoor had identified Grant Hobson as *The Elfin Forest Killer* the same day he was given access to the case files.

The descending elevator was between the third and second floors when McLintock pressed the emergency stop button.

"That case ruined my reputation and my career," McLintock said. "I would have caught Hobson eventually and you were just lucky."

"Alright, you've made your point," Blackmoor said as he reached for the elevator's control panel.

McLintock placed his hand over the ground floor button to prevent Blackmoor from pressing it.

"When I was a young detective, I was forced to interview psychics who claimed to know something about the cases I was working on," McLintock continued. "Especially in cases that were getting a lot of media attention, like unsolved murders or missing children, there was no end of psychics who wanted to get some free publicity. Most psychics are pure con artists but a few actually believe the bullshit they're selling and profilers are no better than psychics who believe their own bullshit."

"I'll report you for this," Blackmoor said.

"Clack was questioned by the police a couple of months ago," McLintock said. "But because he didn't fit your offender profile, the investigating officers didn't think he was a viable suspect. If it hadn't had been for your incorrect profile, Clack might have been arrested and your friends would still be alive."

"Move your hand or I'll move it for you!" Blackmoor threatened. "And while I'm doing it, I'll break your arm!"

"We'll settle it mano a mano soon," McLintock said as he pressed the ground floor button. "But not today."

Blackmoor went home and continued to review the case but after five days he began to wonder if he had been wrong all along and thought perhaps Richard Clack was in fact *The Spectre*. He switched on his TV and instructed it to play anything that had been broadcast on the television or uploaded onto the internet about Richard Clack. His television informed him that since Clack's capture, Clack had been mentioned on news programmes all over the world, three criminologists and four people who knew Clack personally had appeared on chat shows to talk about him, and twenty-five recordings of Clack had been uploaded onto the internet, all of which had received thousands of views. While working as a tour guide in the California forests, Clack had told tall tales around campfires and several people had recorded his anecdotes on their smartphones and had uploaded their recordings of Clack onto the internet; as with most psychopaths, Clack could display an incredible amount of false charm and intelligence and was a very convincing liar. Blackmoor instructed his TV to play the upload of Clack that had received the most views and it played a recording of Clack claiming to have been a Marine Corps Scout Sniper with a hundred and twelve confirmed kills. During his yarn, Clack recited a quote by Ernest Hemingway: *Certainly, there is no hunting like the hunting man and those who have hunted armed men long enough and liked it never really care for anything else thereafter.*

As Clack spoke, Blackmoor had an epiphany and knew exactly what *The Spectre* was going to do next. Over the last five days, Richard Clack had received more media attention than any film star, politician, professional athlete, or rock star and *The Spectre* would be furious that someone else was stealing his thunder. *The Spectre* would like to torture Clack to death slowly but even *The Spectre* would be unable to gain access to Clack while he was in a maximum-security prison. *The Spectre* would believe his next best course of action would be to waylay the two police officers who had arrested Clack and murder them with his signature modus operandi. By doing so, he would prove Clack was a copycat killer and establish *The Spectre* was still at large, he would best the people who had bested Clack and demonstrate his superiority to Clack, and he would embarrass Ramona Cortez and everyone else who had declared Clack to be *The Spectre*.

Blackmoor considered informing Cortez of *The Spectre's* intentions but he knew it would be a pointless exercise as Cortez believed she already had *The Spectre* in custody, but Blackmoor thought he'd better warn Eric Wilson and Virginia Wren, the two police officers who had arrested Clack, that *The Spectre* was hunting them. Blackmoor phoned a friend of his who worked at the same precinct as Wilson and Wren and learnt they had both worked that day and at the end of their shift, Wren had given Wilson a lift to his home; Wilson lived with his girlfriend and Wren would routinely drop him off at his house, on the way to her own home. Blackmoor was given their smartphone numbers but as neither of them answered his calls, he drove to Wilson's house.

On arrival at Wilson's home, Blackmoor saw the lights were on and Wren's car was parked in front of Wilson's house. Blackmoor was about to knock on the front door when he thought it was just possible that *The Spectre* had already ensnared Wilson and Wren and he walked around the house to investigate. Blackmoor entered the backyard and looked through the kitchen window and saw Wilson's pet collie dog was lying on the kitchen floor in a pool of blood and had been shot through the head.

Blackmoor called for police backup with his smartphone and then checked the back door, which he found to be unlocked. He drew his pistol and stealthily entered the house and heard what he thought was someone being beaten with a cane and a man and two women trying to scream with gags in their mouths. The muffled screams were coming from one of the bedrooms and Blackmoor cautiously climbed the stairs. On reaching the bedroom where the muffled screams were coming from, he charged through the doorway with his pistol raised.

Wren and Wilson's girlfriend were both naked and had been tied face down on Wilson's double bed. A man wearing a leather hooded mask, who Blackmoor assumed was *The Spectre*, had been beating them with a riding crop and they both had red stripes crisscrossing their buttocks.

Wilson's wrists and ankles had been manacled and he was sitting in a chair with his back against a wardrobe. A belt had been wrapped around his neck and threaded through the handles of the wardrobe to prevent him from leaving or tipping the chair but allowing him to see everything *The Spectre* was doing to his girlfriend and his partner.

Blackmoor guessed *The Spectre* was concealing his face because he intended to let one of his victims live to testify that he was still at large.

"Freeze!" Blackmoor commanded as he pointed his pistol at *The Spectre*.

Suddenly, *The Spectre* dropped to the floor. Blackmoor got off one shot before *The Spectre* had ducked behind the bed and was shielded by the bodies of the two women and Blackmoor saw a spray of blood as his bullet gouged a furrow across *The Spectre's* back and bored into the wall.

Blackmoor guessed *The Spectre* was reaching for his gun and quickly retreated through the doorway, ran to the stairs, and slid down the carpeted staircase on his back.

The Spectre grabbed his Caledfwlch Assault Carbine and sprayed the walls with gunfire. Blackmoor had heard stories that the rapid fire of a Caledfwlch Assault Carbine could quite literally cut a man in half at the waist. Bullet holes peppered the walls and downstairs ceilings, the windows were shattered, the ground floor lights were smashed, and, through the darkness, scores of narrow beams of light shone through the bullet holes in the downstairs ceilings as the bedroom lights were not smashed. But, miraculously, Blackmoor wasn't shot.

Then the carbine went silent and Blackmoor assumed *The Spectre* was replacing an empty ammunition magazine with a full one. Blackmoor held his pistol in both hands and pointed it at the top of the staircase. He knew that when *The Spectre* appeared at the top of the stairs, he'd only have enough time to fire two or three shots before *The Spectre* located him and shot him to pieces.

Blackmoor waited but *The Spectre* didn't appear and all he could hear were the muffled screams of Wilson, Wren, and Wilson's girlfriend. Blackmoor soon lost patience and stealthily climbed the stairs. On reaching the bedroom, he charged through the doorway but *The Spectre* was not there and Blackmoor guessed he had jumped out of the shattered bedroom window. Blackmoor removed Wilson's gag and Wilson confirmed Blackmoor's supposition.

Chapter Twenty-Two

Blackmoor leaned out of the smashed window and looked for *The Spectre* but he was nowhere to be seen. Blackmoor then started to untie Wren and Wilson's girlfriend and he had removed the gags from their mouths when he heard the police cars arriving, closely followed by the sound of the police entering the house and ascending the stairs. Before the police entered the bedroom, Blackmoor raised his hands as he didn't want to be shot by a zealous police officer.

The police were soon followed by the paramedics, who were soon followed by the crime scene investigators. Wilson, Wren, and Wilson's girlfriend were taken to hospital and Blackmoor was escorted to a police station to make a statement. Blackmoor was interviewed by Cortez and after he'd told her everything that had taken place, he was advised to go home but was assured he'd be informed of any developments in the case.

The next morning, Blackmoor returned to the police station and asked for an update and he was astonished by the answer he received. He was told that DNA tests had been done on the blood samples collected at the crime scene, as *The Spectre* had bled quite a lot from the gunshot wound he'd sustained, and after the blood samples had been tested, crime scene investigators had returned to the crime scene to collect additional blood samples for retesting. Since the additional blood samples had been collected, Ramona Cortez, two crime scene investigators, and the lab tech who conducted blood analysis and DNA testing had locked themselves in the laboratory and were not sharing whatever they had unearthed.

Blackmoor quizzed many of the personnel at the police station to ascertain what the DNA tests had revealed and there was a great deal of speculation. One theory was *The Spectre* was a rich

The Spectre

and powerful man and Cortez was afraid to arrest him. Another supposition was *The Spectre* was a genetically engineered super soldier, probably manufactured by the CIA, who'd gone rogue. The most widely held theory was *The Spectre* was an alien from another planet who'd come to Earth to hunt the men and rape the women. The only supposition that Blackmoor thought could possibly be true was *The Spectre* was a relative of someone who was immensely powerful, like an illegitimate son of the President of the United States that the president didn't even know he had.

At midmorning, Cortez recalled ten members of her disbanded task force and requested they attend a meeting that afternoon, and she also invited Blackmoor and Huxley to the meeting.

Once they were all seated around a conference table, Cortez brought the meeting to order.

"As you're all probably aware, *The Spectre* has resurfaced and has attacked Virginia Wren, Eric Wilson, and Wilson's girlfriend," Cortez said. "Ballistic examination of the slugs fired from the 7.5mm Caledfwlch Assault Carbine at Wilson's home, match the slugs from the attack on Miguel Camacho and his crew in Miami and confirm it's the same weapon and verify that *The Spectre* is still at large and Richard Clack is a copycat killer."

She paused briefly to confirm that everyone present agreed that *The Spectre* was still at large and that Richard Clack was a copycat killer before she continued: "Analysis of blood samples collected at the crime scene revealed *The Spectre* was taking military grade stimulants that gave him superhuman strength and agility."

Cortez had everyone's undivided attention when she started talking about the blood samples collected at Wilson's home as the intriguing mystery surrounding the DNA test results might be revealed.

"We ran repeated DNA tests on multiple blood samples collected from different parts of the crime scene and we found an exact match in the DNA database," Cortez said.

She then paused hesitantly.

Sgt. James Stornoway, a detective in the LAPD Homicide Division, was one of the ten recalled members of her task force and he responded to the tense pause: "I don't care who *The Spectre* is, if you want someone to put their career and pension on the line by arresting him, I'll arrest him."

"Or me! Or me! Or me!" echoed around the room as three other members of her recalled task force passionately volunteered to arrest *The Spectre*.

"The DNA test results have ascertained that *The Spectre* is Geraint Taunton," Cortez said.

Everyone in the room, including Blackmoor, was dumbstruck with surprise.

Eventually, Huxley broke the silence: "Any relation to the Geraint Taunton?"

"It is the Geraint Taunton," Cortez replied.

After an even longer stunned silence, Huxley again spoke: "Geraint Taunton was declared dead by a doctor at the Orange County State Hospital for the Criminally Insane in 2113. When I heard Geraint Taunton was dead, I had to see his body for myself, as did two dozen other law enforcement officers that I'm aware of. An autopsy was performed to establish the cause of death and during the autopsy Taunton's brain was removed as scientists wanted to examine his brain to try and gain insight into what made him a monster. But if Taunton had tricked us all, and he's still alive, he'd be...."

"Ninety-two," Blackmoor interjected, as he'd already done the maths in his head.

"*The Spectre* is very spritely for a ninety-two-year-old," Huxley added.

"It took me all night and most of the morning to make sense of it myself," Cortez replied. "About thirty-five years ago, authorization was given for human cloning."

Cloning is the process of producing a genetically identical copy of an organism. Cloning had started with the replication of laboratory animals and once the process had been perfected, domesticated animals like Thoroughbred racehorses and stud bulls were cloned. Human cloning was illegal, largely because of the risk of creating a human being who was disabled or in poor health from birth, but scientists said they had every reason to believe the process would be one hundred percent successful and in 2099 special permission was given for human cloning. Twenty exceptional people were selected to be cloned, and one, two, three, four, or five clones were made of each of the twenty gene donors, depending on how exceptional they were.

Blackmoor was very well acquainted with the study, as were all psychologists, as it addressed the age-old debate of *nature versus nurture*: whether human behaviour is determined by the genes a person is born with or by childhood experiences.

"Why did they clone a serial killer?" Stornoway asked.

"My guess is they cloned Geraint Taunton because he had a genius level IQ and is widely regarded as the greatest author who ever lived," Cortez replied. "And, as with most serial killers, Taunton had a horrendous childhood and many psychologists believe if he'd had a positive upbringing, he would have used his genius to enrich the world."

Cortez and a few other people around the table looked to Blackmoor for his opinion, and he nodded in agreement.

"It would also account for the secrecy," Cortez continued. "All the clones in the study have received intense public scrutiny and the dread a Geraint Taunton clone would have provoked would have made it difficult if not impossible for him to flourish and his origins would have been kept secret, probably even from the Geraint Taunton clone himself."

"There must be some kind of a record of who the Geraint Taunton clone is," Huxley said.

"There were eight people on the selection committee who chose the people who were to be cloned, but the selection committee was formed thirty-five years ago and now all of its members are deceased," Cortez replied. "The last surviving member of the selection committee was Professor Dean Ambrose, and he died just over a year ago."

"Professor Dean Ambrose was a colleague and a confidant of mine for many years, and I knew him very well indeed," Huxley said. "He strongly believed that if Geraint Taunton had had a positive upbringing, he wouldn't have become a sadistic psychopath and would have used his genius to make the world a better place. I'm certain Dean would have recommended Geraint Taunton as a person to be cloned, and I'm equally as certain that he would have monitored the Geraint Taunton clone very closely and would have kept detailed and extensive records of the study."

Again, Blackmoor nodded in agreement.

"Ambrose left his house and everything else he owned to his housekeeper and I phoned her and asked if she still had any records that had belonged to him," Cortez replied. "His housekeeper told me that shortly after Ambrose died, someone went into his study and took his case files, laptop computers, and memory sticks. She assumed they had been taken by a colleague of his as there was no sign of a break-in, and as nothing valuable had been stolen, she never reported the theft to the police."

"Do you think *The Spectre* found out he was a Geraint Taunton clone and stole Dean's files to conceal his identity?" Huxley asked.

"It's possible," Cortez replied. "It's also possible that *The Spectre* murdered Ambrose. Ambrose died of a heart attack and as he was in his eighties and had a history of heart disease, no one questioned the cause of death, but there are several poisons that can cause a heart attack and *The Spectre* could have murdered Ambrose before stealing his files."

Professor Dean Ambrose had been a close friend of Huxley's for many years and a mentor to Blackmoor for almost as long and they were both visibly shocked by the startling possibility that he had been murdered by *The Spectre.*

Cortez gave the ten recalled members of her task force assignments and ended the meeting, but she asked Blackmoor and Huxley to stay behind after everyone else had gone.

"Will the fact that *The Spectre* is a clone of Geraint Taunton be of any help in catching him?" Cortez asked once they were alone. She asked Huxley because he was the deputy district attorney who had prosecuted Geraint Taunton and she asked Blackmoor because as well as being a criminal profiler, he was also an authority on Geraint Taunton: Blackmoor had read everything ever written by Taunton as well as everything ever written about him. Blackmoor had also collected an assortment of Geraint Taunton memorabilia and the Geraint Taunton collectible he treasured above all the others he owned was a hardcover book written by Geraint Taunton that had been signed by the author. The book was called *The Black, the White, the Blue, and the Gray* and was a historical novel set during the American Civil War. The principal characters of the novel were free black men and escaped slaves who fought in the Union army against the armies of the Confederacy. When Taunton was writing novels, almost all books were published and read on either e-reader, tablet, or laptop, and anything printed on paper inspired the reverence of a Bible, and as *The Black, the White, the Blue, and the Gray* was considered by many academics to be Geraint Taunton's masterpiece, it was published as a hardcover book. Taunton had given an autographed copy of the book to Dean Ambrose, who had given it to Blackmoor on Blackmoor's sixteenth birthday.

"As Geraint Taunton was involved in a car accident as a small child that left his face deformed and scarred, we have no idea what his clone would look like," Blackmoor replied. "In addition to the considerable facial scarring he sustained in the car accident, both of his parents were killed in the crash and the development of Geraint

Taunton's personality was greatly influenced by that traumatic event and I couldn't speculate on the personality of a Geraint Taunton clone who grew up in a different environment."

"Have you anything to add to that?" Cortez asked, addressing her question to Huxley.

"Geraint Taunton's modus operandi was to murder people in their own homes and then torch their houses to obliterate any forensic evidence," Huxley said. "Firefighters kept reporting house fires that were obviously the result of arson and coroners kept informing the police that the burnt bodies recovered from the fires had no soot in their lungs and were dead before the fires were started. Taunton had no affinity with fire other than as a forensic countermeasure, but because fire was part of his signature, the media had nicknamed him *Satan*. His reign of terror went on for over a decade before he was caught, and his capture was the result of a complete fluke."

Blackmoor and Cortez were already familiar with the details of Geraint Taunton's capture: Taunton had invaded a house that a Hollywood film studio was using to accommodate six young female actresses. The house had a steel reinforced security door with a keypad lock but Taunton had clandestinely obtained the five-digit key code and had gained entry to the house with ease.

Once inside the house, he bound and gagged all six of the actresses in one of the bedrooms and had then taken the girl he found most attractive to an adjacent bedroom, where he stripped her naked, tied her face down and spread-eagled to a bed, and had started to flog her with a martinet.

But Taunton was unaware he was being spied on: a voyeur called Derek Chandler had found the six sexy starlets as alluring as had Taunton and had been spying on them with military grade night vision binoculars since nightfall. Chandler had seen Taunton enter the house and, through the windows, had seen him subdue and bind the girls at gunpoint. Taunton had drawn all the curtains before he continued but Chandler had already concluded that the intruder was probably the serial killer known as *Satan* and had used his smartphone to call the police.

While Chandler was still talking to the emergency call operator, a police car arrived, and while he was informing the responding police officers what he had seen, additional police cars arrived. The responding police officers were informed of the five-digit key code of the security door's keypad lock by the film studio's security staff and eight police officers entered the house quietly and with their guns drawn.

Taunton had no idea the police had entered the house until he heard a man saying "Freeze!" and slowly turned and saw two policemen pointing their guns at him.

Once arrested, Taunton denied he was *Satan*. He said he habitually played bondage, domination, and sadomasochistic role-playing games with prostitutes and consensual partners, and his favourite role was the serial killer known as *Satan*, and he claimed the game, and the role had taken him over. Taunton said he was going to play BDSM role-playing games with the six girls but afterwards he planned to give them money and had no intention of raping or murdering them.

The most damning evidence against Taunton was at the time of his arrest, he was in possession of some incendiary devices that were of the same chemical composition as the incendiary devices used by *Satan* to incinerate the houses of his victims, but Taunton claimed he only had them as part of the role he was playing.

Taunton's townhouse, country house, fishing boat, and all his vehicles were thoroughly searched, but no additional incriminating evidence was discovered.

Taunton was a very rich man and he employed the best legal defence team money could buy. Everyone knew it was going to be a long and expensive court case with the possibility that Taunton was only found guilty of six charges of assault and got away with a prison sentence of a few years, or perhaps even a few months. And regardless of the verdict, after the trial, there would be endless speculation as to whether or not Taunton was, in fact, *Satan*, and, if so, how many murders had he actually committed, and the controversy would eclipse the O. J. Simpson trial, the John F. Kennedy assassination, and the Jack the Ripper murders.

Huxley was the only prosecutor who wanted the case and although he was comparatively young and inexperienced, the District Attorney had given it to him.

Huxley met with Taunton and his defence team and negotiated a deal that if Taunton made a full confession, he would spend the rest of his life in the Orange County State Hospital for the Criminally Insane, and not in a maximum-security prison, and he would never be sent to Mexico, Texas or Nevada for trial, where he had also committed some murders and where they still had the death penalty.

Taunton and his defence team said they wanted the agreement in writing and signed by both the District Attorney and the Governor of California.

Once Taunton had the deal in writing, he told Huxley to go to his study where he kept a chess set and said the black queen had been hollowed out, and if he unscrewed the base of the chess piece, he'd find a memory stick inside the black queen which contained a log he'd been keeping since he was sixteen that had detailed accounts of every murder he'd ever committed.

The chess piece was collected and brought to the crime scene investigation laboratory and an investigator unscrewed the base of the black queen and found a memory stick wrapped in tissue paper. Taunton had wrapped the memory stick in tissue paper primarily to cushion it and protect it from damage but also to prevent it from rattling around and revealing there was something hidden in the hollow chess piece.

The investigator plugged the memory stick into a computer and viewed the stored information and Taunton had indeed kept a detailed log of all the murders he'd committed. Taunton had used his smartphone to take pictures of the girls he'd abducted and had photographed and filmed them while they were bound, while they were being tortured, after he'd raped them, and eventually after he'd murdered them, and had downloaded the pictures to his memory stick.

As well as pictures, Taunton had recorded a lot of personal information about the girls he'd murdered, which the police found extremely useful as they were able to identify each and every one of his victims.

Taunton had also chronicled his most intimate thoughts, feelings, desires, experiences, hopes, and ambitions, which he'd written very eloquently as he was an accomplished author.

Blackmoor owned a copy of Taunton's memory stick and had viewed it many times.

Before becoming a recreational murderer, Taunton had studied the techniques used by other serial killers and had learnt the main reason serial killers are caught and convicted is they leave forensic evidence on the bodies of their victims. He reasoned that if his victims' bodies were never found, there would be no forensic evidence. He also reasoned that if the bodies of his victims were never found, the missing person investigations would not become homicide investigations.

To begin with, he dumped the weighted dead bodies of his victims into a deep fishing lake, and later, when he became a rich author, he bought a fishing boat and dumped the weighted bodies into the sea.

Regarding the selection of his victims, Taunton had learnt from a serial killer called Ted Bundy, who only targeted girls he'd never met before, and Taunton only abducted and murdered women who were in no way associated with him and who wouldn't be traced back to him, even as missing persons.

Over a period of almost thirty years, Taunton had abducted, raped, and murdered over two hundred women without being caught or even suspected, but he then changed his modus operandi. He became obsessed with an incredibly attractive forty-three-year-old woman and her two daughters, who were aged twenty and eighteen and were as beautiful as their mother. Taunton wanted to have all three women but abducting three people was almost impossible, and after much deliberation, he decided the only way to have all three of them was to seize them at their own home. One evening, he broke into their house, bound and gagged all three women, and spent the night using them. As a climax to the revelry, Taunton had strangled all three women and, just before leaving, had set fire to their house to obliterate any forensic evidence.

At one time, Taunton had enjoyed abducting his victims, transporting them to his killing rooms, and ultimately disposing of their bodies, but after almost thirty years, he found it to be a bore and a chore, and he decided to continue attacking his victims in their own homes. Although this method alerted the police to the presence of a serial killer, Taunton found the intense media attention gratifying, especially when he'd been given the epithet *Satan*, and he terrorised the Southwest of the United States for over ten years.

"Geraint Taunton was the most evil man I've ever met," Huxley said. "If *The Spectre* is Geraint Taunton back from the dead, he's the Devil incarnate."

Chapter Twenty-Three

Shortly after the meeting with Blackmoor, Huxley, and the recalled members of her task force, Cortez held a press conference and announced that Richard Clack was a copycat killer and *The Spectre* was still at large, but she withheld from the public that *The Spectre* was a clone of Geraint Taunton.

Cortez surmised that as *The Spectre* had hunted down Eric Wilson and Virginia Wren, it was likely *The Spectre* would be coming after Blackmoor and she insisted he have police protection. Blackmoor concurred that *The Spectre* would be coming after him, but he thought it was a certainty and not a likelihood and he proposed they set a trap for *The Spectre* using himself as bait. Cortez agreed to his plan and Blackmoor started wearing a location transmitter that was disguised as a neck pendant, which enabled his police escort to follow him at a distance. The pendant also had an emergency button that would immediately summon his protection squad if pressed.

Blackmoor's gunfight with *The Spectre* received a colossal amount of media attention, all of which glorified Blackmoor and belittled *The Spectre*, which Blackmoor hoped would provoke *The Spectre* into acting without thinking and making mistakes.

For weeks Cortez and her reformed task force followed up on all the new leads but they were still unable to track down *The Spectre*. Blackmoor told Cortez he was convinced that sooner or later *The Spectre* would come after him and all they had to do was wait. They both agreed that *The Spectre's* modus operandi was to attack men when they were in the company of a woman they had some kind of bond with and to add more bait to the trap, Cortez let it be known that she was collaborating with Blackmoor on the case and they were spending time together.

While Blackmoor was involved in the hunt for *The Spectre*, his friend Marty continued to run the self-defence club that Blackmoor had founded. It was Friday evening and Marty was teaching an advanced class that was exclusively for black band students. There were fourteen people taking part in the lesson and the only female attending was Vikki.

The lesson was taking place at a sports centre and an assistant called Larry Boon was stationed at the reception desk. Boon was training to be a fitness instructor and, while in training, was employed by the sports centre as an assistant.

The automatic double doors of the sports centre swung open and a person wearing a hooded leather mask walked in and approached the reception desk Boon was sitting behind. Boon was confused and lost for words for a few seconds and then the stranger in the mask kicked him in the face with a roundhouse kick. Boon was knocked to the floor and he felt the crack as his cheekbone fractured. Then Boon realised the stranger in the mask was *The Spectre*. Boon was trying to get up when *The Spectre* kicked him in the side and broke four of his ribs. Boon rolled across the floor but was still conscious.

The Spectre then walked to the gym where Marty was teaching and barged through the door. Boon managed to get to his feet and with his left hand pressed against his side to support his broken ribs and staggered towards the gym. As he moved towards the gym, he heard a great deal of thudding and screaming. When Boon eventually got to the door and looked in, Marty and everyone he'd been teaching had either been knocked unconscious or were lying on the floor with broken bones. Vikki had been knocked unconscious but apart from that had no visible injuries and *The Spectre* picked her up over his shoulder and started walking towards the door. Boon considered trying to stop him but he thought his best course of action would be to let *The Spectre* pass and remain physically capable of phoning for the police and the paramedics.

Blackmoor and Cortez were at Blackmoor's home when they received a phone call informing them that *The Spectre* had attacked the advanced class of Blackmoor's self-defence club. Blackmoor and Cortez drove to the sports centre, closely followed by Blackmoor's police escort, and when they arrived, the paramedics were in the process of taking the injured to hospital. Police officers at the scene informed Cortez that fifteen people had been injured severely enough to require hospital treatment and Victoria Buchinski had been abducted.

Blackmoor asked to see the list of casualties and saw there were no fatalities.

"*The Spectre* wanted as many witnesses as possible to testify that he'd beaten my entire advanced self-defence class," Blackmoor said to Cortez.

Blackmoor also noticed the person with the most injuries was Marty and surmised that was because Marty kept getting back up to join in the fight, even after he'd been injured.

Toby, Blackmoor's best friend, would attend the advanced self-defence class whenever he wasn't working and Blackmoor was relieved to see that Toby wasn't amongst the list of casualties.

"*The Spectre* must have guessed we were setting a trap for him," Cortez said. "And instead of coming after you directly, he bested your advanced self-defence class and took Victoria Buchinski, your friend with benefits, to celebrate with."

Blackmoor thought that was partially correct but he believed *The Spectre* had abducted Vikki for another reason.

Over the next few days, Cortez and her task force continued to follow up on all the new leads in the investigation and Blackmoor tried to remain stable, even though he could vividly imagine what *The Spectre* was doing to Vikki. To alleviate the frustration and stress he was experiencing, Blackmoor exercised, usually by practising karate combinations on a punching bag, or by sharing his thoughts and feelings with Pippa: his *Dear Diary PC*.

Then five days after her abduction, twenty-one photos of Vikki were emailed to Cortez's task force. Police and forensic investigators examined the photos and learnt they had been taken with and emailed from a disposable phone, commonly referred to as a *burner phone*, and it was unlikely they'd be able to trace its user or its location. In the first photo, Vikki was naked and tied face down to a bed in a spread-eagle position. In the second photo, she had a thin red stripe across her buttocks, suggesting *The Spectre* had given her a single stroke with a cane and then taken a picture. In the next photo, she had two red stripes across her butt and in the picture after that she had three red stripes across her backside and so on until her bottom was crisscrossed with twelve red welts. In the fourteenth photo, Vikki was still naked and tied to the bed in a spread-eagle position but *The Spectre* had flipped her onto her back, implying that he had raped her, or was about to do so, when the picture was taken.

In the fifteenth photo, Vikki was suspended by her wrists in the centre of a well-equipped bondage dungeon and in the following five pictures, she was fettered to a spanking bench, a bondage rack, a Saint Andrew's bondage cross, a bondage wheel, and a trestle. In the last photo, she was locked in a cage that was about the size of a dog kennel.

In all the photos where Vikki was looking at the camera and at *The Spectre* who was taking the pictures, there was no fear on her face, just hate, but in many of the photos, she had tears on her cheeks.

Blackmoor forced himself to look at the pictures and he and Cortez both agreed *The Spectre* was taunting him.

It was close to midnight on Friday evening (seven days after *The Spectre* had abducted Vikki) and Blackmoor was talking with Pippa.

"I keep getting the idea that I'd met *The Spectre* before I encountered him at Eric Wilson's home," Blackmoor said.

"*The Spectre* is a clone of Geraint Taunton, who you've studied very extensively, and perhaps that's why you think, or feel, that you've met him before," Pippa replied.

"That's possible," Blackmoor said. "But I can't get it out of my head that I've met *The Spectre* in another context."

"Perhaps he approached you as a client or as a colleague, or he may have been introduced to you by a mutual acquaintance," Pippa suggested.

After a few minutes of cogitation, Blackmoor responded to Pippa's suggestion: "Two men come to mind: Jack Smith and George Claridge."

"How did you meet them?" Pippa asked.

"Toby had asked me to help him move some gear that a camping and outdoor equipment store had donated to a homeless shelter and Jack Smith had helped us load the gear into a truck and unload it at the homeless shelter," Blackmoor replied. "He claimed to be a gambling addict who'd been forced to go into hiding after he'd embezzled money from his employer to fuel his gambling addiction."

"As a result of your encounter with *The Spectre*, you know his height and build," Pippa said. "And as he's a clone of Geraint Taunton and the cloning experiment took place in 2099, you know *The Spectre's* age to within a few months. Is Jack Smith the right height, build, and age to be *The Spectre*?" Pippa didn't ask who Toby was as Blackmoor had spoken of him on many previous occasions.

"Yes," Blackmoor said. "He's the right height, build, and age to be *The Spectre*, and when I met him, I was surprised at how much strength and stamina he had for someone who was homeless."

"And how did you meet George Claridge?" Pippa asked.

"He approached me as a client and claimed to be a necrophiliac who'd worked as an undertaker to gain access to dead bodies," Blackmoor replied.

Blackmoor was about to contact Cortez to ask her to investigate Jack Smith and George Claridge when he received the text message he'd been expecting: *Lose your police escort and text me when you've shaken them off. If you don't come alone, I'll post you some of Victoria's body parts.* The text message was accompanied by some additional photos of Vikki to prove it was from *The Spectre*.

Blackmoor had anticipated the message and had already formulated a plan. He was already wearing a tracksuit and gym shoes, which would be to his advantage if he had to fight *The Spectre* as he would need to be quick on his feet, and, as well as his pistol, Blackmoor took a pepper spray that blinded temporarily, which he tucked into his sock. He chose a pepper spray as his backup weapon because it was made exclusively of plastic and if *The Spectre* forced him to walk through a metal detector door scanner, the pepper spray wouldn't trigger the alarm.

Blackmoor was being used as bait to lure *The Spectre* into a trap and his police escort kept a discreet distance as they didn't want to alert *The Spectre* of their presence and were stationed in an empty house two streets away from Blackmoor's home. Consequently, all Blackmoor had to do to elude his protection squad was to remove the neck pendant that housed a location transmitter, which kept him in contact with them. Once he'd done so, Blackmoor texted *The Spectre* and informed him he'd eluded his police escort and his smartphone rang almost immediately. Blackmoor answered the call and a voice that was distorted by a disguiser microphone spoke to him: "Go to the front entrance of *Wollstonecraft's Shopping Mall* and await further instructions."

Blackmoor got into his car and instructed the self-drive computer to take him to the shopping precinct. On arrival, he parked his car and walked to the mall, which was now closed, and, on reaching the front entrance, he received a phone call. Blackmoor answered the call and *The Spectre* gave him his next instruction: "Come in."

As *The Spectre* spoke, the electronically controlled front doors of the mall clicked open. Blackmoor surmised that *The Spectre* was in the mall's security control room and was observing him with the

The Spectre

mall's CCTV surveillance cameras. He considered calling for help but he knew if the police didn't catch *The Spectre, The Spectre* would carry out his threat to post him some of Vikki's body parts and Blackmoor decided he couldn't take the chance.

Blackmoor entered the mall and the doors locked behind him. There was a long straight walkway that was thirty to forty feet wide and on either side of the walkway were lines of shops. The walkway was illuminated but the shops were closed and in darkness and halfway along the walkway was a fountain.

"Throw your pistol into the fountain," *The Spectre* said.

Blackmoor walked to the fountain and threw his pistol into the water. He also took off his jacket and shoulder holster, both of which he dropped to the floor.

"Throw your smartphone into the fountain and take the escalator to the upper floor," *The Spectre* said.

Beyond the fountain on the same long straight walkway was a large glass display cabinet currently displaying crystal glassware and on either side of the display cabinet were escalators: one going up and one coming down.

Blackmoor threw his smartphone into the water, walked to the escalators, and rode the moving staircase to the upper floor.

Most of the upper floor was in darkness but an area in front of the escalators that was about the size of a tennis court was illuminated and empty. Blackmoor guessed that was where *The Spectre* wanted to fight him.

At the very edge of the illuminated area, Vikki was tied to a chair. She was only wearing a bra and panties and *The Spectre* had strapped a ball gag in her mouth.

As Blackmoor walked towards her, *The Spectre* emerged from the shadows. He was dressed exclusively in black and was wearing a hooded leather mask.

The Spectre was a clone of Geraint Taunton and was every one of Blackmoor's heroes and demons rolled into one.

Blackmoor didn't adopt a guard stance as he didn't want to lose the element of surprise and he attacked *The Spectre* from a standing position with a combination of kicks and punches. *The Spectre* moved backwards but blocked or evaded every one of Blackmoor's strikes. Blackmoor continued to attack with various techniques and combinations of techniques but *The Spectre* was toying with him.

The Spectre concluded their first clash by punching Blackmoor in the face and knocking him to the floor.

The Spectre then walked away and gave Blackmoor time to recover.

Blackmoor had a deep cut over his left eye that would require sutures (if he lived) and blood was running down his face.

Blackmoor was aware that *The Spectre* could have killed him, maimed him, or knocked him unconscious but chose to give him time to recover. Blackmoor guessed that *The Spectre* was furious about their encounter at Eric Wilson's home and was even more enraged by the biased media attention they had both received and intended to toy with him like a cat playing with a mouse. Blackmoor also guessed that *The Spectre* was recording their fight via the mall's surveillance cameras and was going to put the recording of their contest on the internet to gain the terror and awe he craved, which would explain why he was wearing a mask.

As Blackmoor got to his feet, he thought it unlikely he could beat a Geraint Taunton clone even if the Geraint Taunton clone hadn't taken stimulants, and as *The Spectre* had taken military grade pharmaceuticals that gave him superhuman strength and agility, and even sharpened his reflexes, Blackmoor didn't know what his next move would be. He'd already tried a surprise attack and had employed all his most practiced and proven techniques and had made no impression on *The Spectre*, and Blackmoor strongly regretted not calling for help when he had the chance.

Blackmoor again attacked with combinations of kicks and hand strikes and *The Spectre* again blocked and evaded all his techniques before counterattacking with a spinning back kick that hit Blackmoor in the face and knocked him to the floor. Blackmoor's lips were torn against his teeth and his mouth quickly filled with blood.

As Blackmoor started to get up, *The Spectre* placed his hands under Blackmoor's armpits from behind, picked him up, and threw him through the air like a rag doll, and he crashed through the front window of one of the closed shops.

Blackmoor gathered *The Spectre* was still performing for the cameras.

Blackmoor had one last card left to play: as he clambered to his feet amongst the fragments of broken window glass in the dark shadows of the closed shop, Blackmoor surreptitiously removed the pepper spray from his sock and concealed it in his clenched right fist.

Blackmoor walked out of the shop and when he was about five feet away from *The Spectre*, fired the pepper spray into his face. The stimulants *The Spectre* had taken were also powerful painkillers and he didn't feel the sting in his eyes and realise Blackmoor was armed with a pepper spray until he was blind.

The Spectre closed his eyes and rushed at Blackmoor. Blackmoor knew *The Spectre* could literally tear him limb from limb if he got hold of him and he jumped to one side and tried to find a gap in *The Spectre's* guard that would enable him to land a death blow. Blackmoor repeatedly evaded *The Spectre's* lunges and every time he moved, *The Spectre* pinpointed his position, adopted a guard stance to defend himself, and rushed forwards.

Blackmoor knew the odds were still not in his favour and in desperation he threw the pepper spray to his left side. As the pepper spray hit the floor, *The Spectre* heard it bounce and turned to face where he thought Blackmoor had jumped. As he did so, he opened his guard, and Blackmoor spun on the spot and landed a back kick in *The Spectre's* chest, which catapulted *The Spectre* over the upper floor's safety barrier. *The Spectre* didn't scream as he fell from the upper floor and the short eerie silence was suddenly broken by the deafening sound of glass shattering as *The Spectre* crashed into the display cabinet that was between the escalators and directly below the safety barrier.

Blackmoor looked over the safety barrier and *The Spectre* was lying motionless amongst the debris of the shattered display cabinet and the crystal glassware it was exhibiting. A pool of blood slowly appeared around *The Spectre* and the blood pool gradually expanded.

Once Blackmoor was satisfied *The Spectre* was neutralised, he went to free Vikki. He started to untie her, beginning with the ball gag, but *The Spectre* had used some very complicated knots and numerous pieces of rope. Blackmoor would have looked for a knife to cut the ropes, or for a phone to call for help, but he didn't want to leave Vikki tied to the chair.

Once Vikki realised *The Spectre* was dead and the nightmare was over, she could easily have broken down in floods of tears, but she forced herself to retain her composure.

When *The Spectre* regained consciousness, he was weak from blood loss. He reached into his pocket and retrieved a pill box that contained his military grade stimulants and poured the full contents of the pill box into his mouth. The tablets dissolved as soon as they made contact with the blood and saliva in his mouth and he easily swallowed them. His vision was still dark and blurry but he could hear the fountain and he could just about make out its silhouette. *The Spectre* got to his feet and walked towards the fountain with the intention of washing the pepper spray out of his eyes.

As he walked, he began to feel light-headed and the dizziness preceded a blackout.

When *The Spectre* regained his senses, he was standing in the fountain with his face under the cascading water and he guessed the massive dose of stimulants he'd taken had caused him to have an absence seizure. He wasn't sure how long he'd been standing with his face under the cascading water but his vision was a lot clearer and he planned to collect his carbine, which he'd hidden in one of the closed shops, and kill Blackmoor and Victoria.

The Spectre again started to feel light-headed and the dizziness preceded another absence seizure. When he recovered from the absence seizure, he was holding his carbine and riding the escalator to the upper floor, although he had no recollection of retrieving his carbine or boarding the escalator.

Finally, Blackmoor had unpicked all the knots and freed Vikki.

"Let's find a phone and call for help," Blackmoor said.

"I want to see him dead," Vikki replied.

Blackmoor and Vikki walked to the safety barrier and looked over. When they saw there was a lot of blood but no body, they quickly turned and saw *The Spectre* pointing his carbine at them.

Just then, *The Spectre* again started to feel dizzy. Before he lost touch with reality, he fired his carbine and sprayed bullets at Blackmoor and Victoria at chest level. Bullets tore through their hearts and lungs and they fell to the floor.

The Spectre had a third blackout and when he regained his senses, he was sitting on the floor with his back against the safety barrier that Blackmoor had kicked him over. He looked up and Blackmoor and Victoria were standing over him and Victoria was holding his carbine.

"I killed you both," *The Spectre* said.

"Only in your sick, twisted, drug-crazed mind," Blackmoor replied. "You're bleeding to death; you'll be dead before the paramedics get here."

The Spectre evaluated what Blackmoor had said to him for about ten seconds, and then he died.

Chapter Twenty-Four

Blackmoor and Vikki went to the mall's security control room with the primary intention of finding a phone, and while Vikki was calling for help, Blackmoor switched on every light in the mall and opened the front doors. One of the mall's security guards had left his uniform jacket on the back of a chair and as Vikki was half naked, she put the jacket on and rolled up the sleeves. The jacket fitted her like a baggy mini dress and Blackmoor mused to himself that she looked like one of Braeburn's models.

Braeburn was a photographer, who was famous enough to be known by just one name, and one of his many tricks was to photograph his models wearing men's clothing that was too big for them, which made his models look both vulnerable and protected.

Within minutes of Vikki making the phone call, police officers and paramedics were entering the mall. A paramedic put a dressing on the wound above Blackmoor's left eye and she urged Blackmoor to be taken to hospital to be examined by a doctor and to have the wound sutured. Blackmoor agreed he needed to be taken to hospital but said he wouldn't leave without Vikki, who also needed to be examined by a doctor.

Blackmoor searched for Vikki and when he located her, she was having a discussion with Cortez and Stornoway.

Just then, Blackmoor noticed the coroner was taking *The Spectre's* body away and a crime scene investigator was carrying *The Spectre's* hooded leather mask in a transparent plastic evidence bag. Blackmoor was curious to know who *The Spectre* was and as he walked towards *The Spectre's* body, which was in a body bag and on a gurney, Cortez and Vikki hurriedly intercepted him.

"*The Spectre* was carrying identification and his name is Rex Whitby," Cortez said. "Your offender profile of him was incredibly accurate and he was a successful and powerful international businessman. He was a self-made millionaire before he was twenty-one and a multi-billionaire before he was twenty-five. He owned an international commercial airline and had a pilot's licence and he could get from anywhere in the world to anywhere in the world without leaving a trail, which is why he never appeared anywhere in our investigation."

"I might have met him while he was using another name," Blackmoor said. "I want to see his face."

Cortez and Vikki fell silent.

"He's going to find out sooner or later," Stornoway said.

After a pensive pause, Cortez responded: "I think later would have been better than sooner, but now he's asked, the not knowing would be torture."

Cortez stepped aside and instructed the coroner to let Blackmoor see *The Spectre's* face.

Blackmoor unzipped the body bag, flipped back the flap, and looked at the face of *The Spectre*: the Geraint Taunton clone: the Devil incarnate.

The shock hit Blackmoor like a bolt of lightning, and he staggered backwards, fell to the floor, and landed in a sitting position.

As he looked at the face of *The Spectre*, it was like looking at an identical twin brother, and Blackmoor realised he was also a Geraint Taunton clone.

THE END